"Why do  **man?" Ja**

"Don't ya wa_____ cherish you?"

She flashed him a look, startled by the intensity of his golden gaze. Cherish? She was hoping for someone who would be happy to have her to wife. She would feel blessed to be cherished by her husband, but she doubted that would ever happen.

"Younger men don't want me." Annie felt her face heat. "I can trust an older man."

"What about me?" Jacob asked.

"You? What about you?"

"Don't you trust me?"

Annie grew flustered as she felt his gaze. "I trust you," she hedged, wondering where the conversation was leading. "We are friends—" He shifted in his seat, and Annie saw him wince. "I'm sorry. Your hand is hurting you."

"I'm fine," he insisted, but his pale features said otherwise.

Was Jacob actually suggesting that she consider him as someone who could be more than a friend? Had he been serious? Testing her? Teasing her? Now that he had put the idea in her mind, she had trouble dismissing it. They were friends, she reminded herself.

Rebecca Kertz was first introduced to the Amish when her husband took a job with an Amish construction crew. She enjoyed watching the Amish foreman's children at play and swapping recipes with his wife. Rebecca resides in Delaware with her husband and dog. She has a strong faith in God and feels blessed to have family nearby. Besides writing, she enjoys reading, doing crafts and visiting Lancaster County.

Books by Rebecca Kertz

Love Inspired

Lancaster County Weddings Series

Noah's Sweetheart
Jedidiah's Bride
A Wife for Jacob

Visit the Author Profile page at Harlequin.com for more titles

A Wife for Jacob

Rebecca Kertz

Recycling programs
for this product may
not exist in your area.

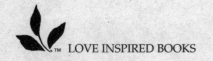

LOVE INSPIRED BOOKS

ISBN-13: 978-0-373-87943-4

A Wife for Jacob

Copyright © 2015 by Rebecca Kertz

All rights reserved. Except for use in any review, the reproduction
or utilization of this work in whole or in part in any form by any
electronic, mechanical or other means, now known or hereinafter
invented, including xerography, photocopying and recording, or in
any information storage or retrieval system, is forbidden without
the written permission of the editorial office, Love Inspired Books,
233 Broadway, New York, NY 10279 U.S.A.

This is a work of fiction. Names, characters, places and incidents are
either the product of the author's imagination or are used fictitiously, and
any resemblance to actual persons, living or dead, business establishments,
events or locales is entirely coincidental.

This edition published by arrangement with Love Inspired Books.

® and TM are trademarks of Love Inspired Books, used under license.
Trademarks indicated with ® are registered in the United States Patent
and Trademark Office, the Canadian Intellectual Property Office and in
other countries.

www.Harlequin.com

Printed in U.S.A.

Beloved, let us love one another, for love is of God;
and everyone who loves is born of God
and knows God.
—*1 John* 4:7

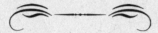

For my dearest husband,
whom I love with all of my heart…
I feel blessed that I met and married you.

Chapter One

Lancaster County, Pennsylvania

The windows were open, allowing the warm breeze of early autumn to flow throughout the two-story farmhouse. Anna Zook sat in the family gathering room, folding laundry from a basket of line-dried clothes. She pulled out her youngest brother Peter's light blue shirt, held it up for inspection and then laid it across the back of the sofa.

It was quiet. Her mother, Peter and her sister Barbara had taken her grandparents up north to see her *grossmudder's* sister, Evie, in New Wilmington, an Amish community north of Pittsburgh. Her older brother Josiah had left early this morning to visit the Amos Kings, most particularly his new sweetheart, Nancy. *Dat* was making some repairs to the *grosseldre's* house while her grandparents were away.

As she reached into the basket for another garment, Annie glanced at Millie, sleeping on the floor not far from her feet. Every day she thanked the Lord that *Dat* allowed her to keep her dog inside the house instead of out in the barn where the other animals were kept. In her community, most pets were excluded from homes, but Millie was special, at least to Annie. And her father was kind to understand what Millie meant to her.

She spread an apron on the cushion beside her, smoothing out the wrinkles before laying it on top of Peter's shirt. Millie lifted her head and eyed Annie briefly before closing her eyes and lying back down. Annie smiled tenderly at the animal. Millie was a black-and-white mongrel—"mutt" Peter called her—with soulful brown eyes and a mouth that looked as if she were smiling whenever she sat up, panting for a treat. She loved Millie; the dog gave her unconditional affection, following her wherever she went. It had been Millie who had helped her get over the heartache and loss of Jedidiah Lapp. When he'd talked of being friends, she'd known he was telling her that he was no longer interested in her as his sweetheart.

I'll not be hurt again, she thought. Only by marrying for practical reasons would she keep her heart safe. *I'll wed a church elder or a widower with children, someone who will appreciate me and be happy to have me as his bride.* Then after the wedding, she would learn to become fond of her husband. No handsome young man would hurt her again.

As she folded pants, socks and undergarments, Annie frowned. Lately, her mother had been hinting that she wasn't getting any younger. "You should find someone to marry and soon," *Mam* had said.

How could she find someone to marry? Didn't they have to show an interest in her first? She tried to think of all the older men who were free to marry. Preacher Levi Stoltzfus. Amos King's brother Ike, newly back in his home community from Indiana, where he'd lived with his wife before she'd passed on.

Annie loved it in Happiness. Whomever she married must stay here. Charlotte King had married Abram Peachy, their deacon, and she was happy raising Abram's five children. *If I can find someone as nice as Abram, I'll be content.* First respect, then love will follow, a safe kind of love that brings only peace rather than heartbreak.

She picked up a stack of socks and set them carefully in the laundry basket. Next to the socks, she placed the folded undergarments. Suddenly, Millie rose up on all fours and began to bark fiercely.

"Millie!" she scolded, startled by her dog's behavior. "Stop that this minute!" What was bothering her?

But the dog continued to bark as she scurried toward the window, rose up on her hind legs, propped her front paws on the windowsill and then barked and whined as she peered outside.

"Girl, what do you see?" Annie frowned as she approached, looking over the dog's head to search the yard for the cause of the animal's agitation. And she saw the ladder against the *grosseldre's* house leaning crookedly against the gutter. Suddenly apprehensive, Annie searched for her father and then saw him, lying on the ground not far from the base of the ladder.

"Dat!" She rushed out of the house and ran to him. Millie slipped out behind her, but Annie cared only to get to her father to see if he was all right. Millie hovered nearby, wanting to get close enough to sniff *Dat*, and Annie had to scold the young dog to stay away.

"Dat," Annie breathed as she knelt near his head.

He groaned. "Annie—" He tried to rise and cried out with pain.

"Nay," she said. "Don't move. We don't know how badly you're hurt."

Her father lay with his eyes closed, looking paler than

she'd ever seen him. "I'll go for help. Stay where you are." She leaned closer. "*Dat*, can you hear me?"

"*Ja,*" came his soft whisper, then he grimaced.

Annie stood, and raced barefoot through the grass and down the dirt drive as fast as she could, her heart thudding, her fear rising with each step. It wasn't safe to try to move him herself. She had to get help.

"We had a *gut* morning," Jacob Lapp said as he steered the family's horse-driven market wagon from Bird-in-Hand toward home. "*Dat* will be pleased that we picked up the lumber."

"*Ja*, and *Mam* will be happy we bought everything on her list and so quickly," his younger brother Isaac said.

Jacob flashed him a glance. "You helping *Dat* with the repairs at Abram's?"

"*Ja*, 'tis why he wanted the lumber this morning. The shed on the deacon's property has become unsafe. Abram is afraid that one of the children will get hurt."

Jacob silently agreed. A building that wasn't sturdy was an accident waiting to happen. "They'll have plenty of time to fix the shed today," he said conversationally. "It's a *gut* day to be working outside." His brothers were handy with tools, expert in construction. Jacob could handle a hammer as well as any of them, but he didn't want to work in that occupation for a living.

He sighed. He wanted what his older brothers had: a wife, a home and work that would provide for his family. His older brothers had found their life paths. Noah was an expert cabinetmaker with a thriving business. Jedidiah, his eldest brother, owned a small farm and supplemented his income with construction work when it suited him.

But me? I help Dat with the farmwork, but I don't want to be a farmer, nor do I want to work in construc-

tion. And I don't have Noah's talent for making furniture. He had no idea what his special God-given gifts were, and until he discovered he had any, he'd not be thinking of marrying. He wouldn't wed until he could provide for a family.

As he drove down the main road, past Whittier's Store, and continued on, Jacob pushed those thoughts aside and enjoyed the scenery. The only sounds were the horse's hooves hitting pavement and the occasional rev of an engine as a car approached and then passed.

Suddenly, he saw a young Amish woman running barefoot down the road. She stopped and waved at them frantically as they drove past. *"Schtupp!"*

Jacob pulled the buggy to the side of the road. Once he'd reined the horse to a halt, he sprang from the vehicle and hurried back to see what was wrong. He recognized the young woman immediately. "Annie!" She was Annie Zook, a friend from childhood and his brother Jed's former sweetheart.

Annie hesitated. "Jacob?"

"Ja." He studied her with concern. "Annie, is something wrong? Can we help?"

She glanced from him to Isaac as if she wondered if they could help. *"Dat's* hurt!" she exclaimed. "He fell off the roof of my *grosseldre's* house!"

Jacob hid his alarm. "Is he conscious?"

"Ja," she cried, "but he's in pain!"

"I'll stay with you," he told her, "while Isaac goes for help." Isaac climbed out of the vehicle and approached. Jacob addressed his younger brother, "I'll drive to the Zooks', then you take the wagon. Find a phone and call 911." Isaac nodded, his expression turning anxious before he got back into the vehicle. Jacob helped Annie into the buggy, then he climbed in and took up the leathers. *"Yah!"* he cried, spurring the horse on.

The horse's hooves pounded against the macadam road. Jacob drove down the dirt lane to the Zooks' farmhouse, hopped out and helped Annie to alight. He turned to his brother. "Hurry, Isaac!" he urged. "Try the Martins or Whittier's Store."

"I will." Isaac slid over and grabbed the reins. "Don't worry, Annie. I'll get help." Then, he set the mare to a fast pace as he steered the animal back to the main road and toward the nearest available phone.

"Where is your *vadder*?" Jacob asked.

"Over here," she said. He accompanied her past the main house to where her father had fallen.

Jacob felt his heart beat faster as he saw the ladder, which looked like it would topple over. He noted the danger to Joe, who lay on the ground a few feet away. "Hold on, Joe!" He rushed to move the piece of equipment a safe distance from the *dawdi haus* before he returned quickly to hunker down near the injured man's head. "Joe?" he said softly. His fear rose when the man didn't immediately respond.

"Dat!" Annie sobbed, clearly terrified. *"Dat*, open your eyes—say something! *Please!"* She touched her father's cheek. *"Dat*, Jacob Lapp is here. Isaac has gone for help."

Joe's eyelashes fluttered and then opened. "Annie?"

Annie crouched next to Jacob. *"Ja, Dat!* Jacob and me. What hurts?"

"My leg," he gasped.

Joe tried to rise, then cried out and reached toward his left leg. Jacob immediately stopped him. *"Nay.* Don't move. You could injure yourself more."

Joe leaned back and closed his eyes. "Burns," he whispered. "Feels like fire."

"Hold on." Jacob's gaze met Annie's. "An ambulance will be here soon," he assured her.

Her blue eyes glistening with tears, she nodded. "I didn't know what to do."

"You did the right thing, leaving him be to get help." Jacob felt a little catch as he studied her. He'd never seen her looking so vulnerable. He rose to his feet and offered her his hand. She appeared reluctant to take it and rose without help.

It seemed like forever, but it must have been only ten minutes till they heard the ambulance siren. Jacob managed a smile. "Help has come."

"Thanks be to God," she prayed. He could see that she was trying to pull herself together.

The ambulance drove closer, rumbling over the dirt lane toward the house. "It was just you and Horseshoe Joe home?" Jacob asked softly, using the nickname that Annie's father went by in the community.

"*Ja. Grossmudder* and *Grossdaddi* wanted to visit family in New Wilmington. *Mam*, Barbara and Peter went with them."

"And Josiah?"

Watching as the ambulance pulled into the yard and stopped, Annie hugged herself with her arms. "At the Kings. He left to see Nancy early this morning."

"When Isaac comes, I'll send him to tell your brother." Jacob noted her shiver and studied her with a frown. "Are you cold?"

"*Nay,*" she whispered. "I'm fine."

He could see that she wasn't, but he kept silent. Jacob glanced downward and saw blood along the side of her left foot. "You're hurt!" he exclaimed, upset for not noticing before.

"'Tis nothing," she assured him.

The ambulance had stopped, and three men climbed out of the vehicle. Jacob approached to explain the situation to them and then took the men to Joe before he returned to Annie. "You should have someone look at your foot."

"Nay—"

"Let me see it," he said firmly. She seemed taken aback by his brusqueness, but she obeyed and raised her left foot. He hissed at what he saw. "Now the other one." The right foot looked as bad as the left. The bottoms of both her feet were scratched and bleeding; the soles looked angry and sore. "What did you do to yourself?" he said gently. Running barefoot, she must have stepped on broken glass.

"Dat fell. I couldn't worry about shoes!" she cried, almost angrily.

Jacob nodded. "I know. I would have done the same thing. But now that your father is getting help, you must take care of yourself. Your *dat* is going to need you. You don't want to get an infection and be ill, do *you*?"

His words seemed to calm her. She sniffed as she met his gaze. *"Nay."*

"I'll run inside and get something for you to wear on your feet." He turned to leave. "I'll just speak with these men first to see if they can take a quick look—"

"Jacob!" Annie's call stopped him in his strides.

He spun back. *"Ja?"*

"Don't bother the men. They're helping *Dat.* I can wait. You'll find black socks in the laundry basket in my *grosseldre's* kitchen. I did their laundry but haven't put it away yet." She gestured toward her grandparents' cottage. "And my *grossmudder's* old sneakers are by the back door. We wear the same size shoe. I can wear those."

Jacob studied her, noting the anxiety playing on her lovely features, the look of fear in her glistening blue eyes. Tendrils of blond hair had escaped from beneath her white prayer *kapp*. She wore a full-length black apron over a lavender dress. Jacob noticed the way her bottom lip quivered, as if she was ready to break down and cry. But she didn't. She remained strong.

"I'll get you the socks," he said softly. Inside the *dawdi haus*, he found the pair of socks right where she told him they would be. He grabbed them and the navy sneakers, brought them outside and handed them to her. "Your *dat's* in *gut* hands, Annie. These men know what they're doing." She nodded. "They'll get him to the hospital. You'll need to go there, as well."

"Ja," she said, glancing toward where the men bent over her father. She held on to the socks he'd given her but made no effort to put them on.

"Do you need help?" he asked quietly.

"Nay. I can do it." But she didn't move. She watched the men working on her father.

"Annie," he said. "Do *you* need help?" Without waiting for her answer, Jacob gently took the socks from her and hunkered down near her feet. "Hold on to my shoulder."

He tried not to think about the fact that he was holding Annie's bare foot as he carefully pulled on the first sock and then the second one. Within seconds, he felt satisfied that her injured feet would be protected. He rose and, without meeting her glance as she bent to put on the shoes, turned to watch the ambulance workers.

As two men lifted Joe onto a stretcher, the driver approached them. "Are you relatives?" he asked.

"*I* am," Annie said as she straightened. "I'm his daughter."

"We've secured his neck in a brace, and we've done what we could for him. It looks like he may have fractured his leg. We'll be taking him to General Hospital. They'll do X-rays and check for other injuries." The dark-haired man wore a white shirt and pants and a white jacket embroidered with the red insignia of the ambulance company. "Do you want to ride with us?" he asked Annie.

She hesitated. "*Ja.*"

"That's fine," Jacob said. "We'll make sure Josiah gets to the hospital."

A car rumbled down the dirt drive and stopped near the main farmhouse. As Jacob approached the vehicle, the door on the driver's side opened and Bob Whittier stepped out. "Isaac called from the store," he said. "Rick Martin was there. Your brother told us what happened." He paused, studied the scene. "Do you need a lift to the hospital?"

Jacob shot Annie a quick glance. "Annie's going in the ambulance with Joe. I'll take the ride." The kind *Englisher* nodded and Jacob returned to Annie's side. "I'm going to follow behind the ambulance with Bob."

Annie didn't seem pleased. "You don't have to come."

"*Ja,* I do. You shouldn't be alone." He paused. "I'll stay until your brother gets there." He watched as the EMTs carefully shifted Joe onto a stretcher. "Looks like they're getting ready to move him."

"I need to get my purse," she said.

"Where's Isaac?" Jacob asked Bob as Annie hurried toward the farmhouse.

"Rick is taking him to the Kings to tell Josiah what

happened. As soon as he can, Rick will bring them to the hospital."

Annie returned with purse in hand, and Jacob stood beside her and Bob as the EMTs placed Joe carefully into the back of the vehicle. He heard Annie's sharp little inhalation, and he felt the strongest desire to comfort her, tell her that Joe would be all right and she had no reason to worry, except that he didn't know the extent of her father's injuries. He settled a hand on her shoulder and felt her jerk as if startled. He drew his fingers away.

One of the ambulance workers approached. "We're ready to go."

"I'm coming," she said.

Jacob couldn't help himself from reaching for her hand, just for a moment, to give it a reassuring squeeze. She broke away and hurried toward the ambulance. The memory of her shocked look stayed with him as he climbed into the front seat of Bob's car and buckled his seat belt. They were nearly at the hospital when he heard the light toot of a car horn behind them. He glanced back to see Rick's car. He was glad that the *Englisher* was able to bring Josiah so quickly.

He could tell Bob to turn around and take him back. Annie didn't want him at the hospital. But she would just have to tolerate his presence. He wasn't about to go home without learning if Joe was all right. It was the correct thing to do.

"Your father needs surgery. He has a displaced fracture of the tibia and fibula in his left leg, the two bones that make up the shin. He hit his head when he fell, but I don't think that injury is severe. Looks like the leg suffered the worst of it. We'll do a CT scan to be certain. He'll need surgery to repair the damage."

Annie nodded. "Will he be all right?" Her fear rose with each revelation the doctor made.

"There are no guarantees, but his prognosis looks good. We're running tests to make sure an underlying condition didn't cause his fall, but from what your father told me, I don't believe that's the case."

"When can we see him?" Josiah asked.

Annie glanced at her brother, who was frowning. He looked impatient, agitated.

In direct contrast, Dr. Moss looked confident and competent in her white lab coat. "You can see him for a few minutes before we take him up to surgery," she said. A nurse approached with a clipboard. "Excuse me." Dr. Moss studied the chart and nodded. She spoke privately with the young woman before she returned her attention to Josiah and Annie. "I'll need one of you to sign a consent form."

While her brother waited for the form, Annie flashed Jacob a glance. She was keenly aware of his presence. When their gazes caught, she looked away. Why had he come? He said that he'd stay only until her brother arrived, but Josiah had arrived the same time as Jacob. She wanted him to leave. But how could she make him go after the way he'd helped with *Dat*? He cared about her father and she had to respect his feelings. She recalled the image of young twelve-year-old Jacob hanging on to her father's every word as her *dat* taught him about blacksmithing.

Disturbed by the memory, she tried to focus on Josiah, now bent over a clipboard with pen in hand. But she remained acutely aware of the man behind her. She glanced at him out of the corner of her eye. She was relieved to see him deep in conversation with his brother Isaac, Bob Whittier and Rick Martin.

Tall, with dark hair like his eldest brother Jacob wore a royal blue shirt with suspenders holding up his *triblend* denim pants. He held his black-banded straw hat in his hands. She dared to examine his face. His features were a beautiful combination of his *mam* and *dat*—Katie and Samuel Lapp. Annie scowled and Jacob turned, caught her gaze. She gasped, looked away. How embarrassing to be caught staring. To her dismay, she sensed his approach.

"Are you all right?" Jacob asked softly.

She shook her head. "I will be once I know my father is all right."

"He spoke to us," he said. "That's a *gut* sign." He offered her an encouraging smile. "I'm praying for his quick recovery."

Tears sprang to Annie's eyes. "I appreciate that." It was a kind thing for him to say, but then Jacob had been kind to her from the first moment he'd jumped out of his buggy and offered his help. And she'd been anything but kind to him.

A nurse appeared from behind them. "You may see your father now but only for a few minutes. We'll be taking him up to surgery shortly. Only immediate family may see him."

"Thank you," Annie said. She turned to Jacob. "I'll let you know how he is as soon as I can. I don't want to keep you."

Jacob smiled. Amusement flashed in his golden eyes. "You're not keeping me from anything. I'll wait for you."

"I won't be long," she said as she turned away.

"Annie," Josiah interrupted, "we have to go now, or we'll miss our chance to see *Dat*."

She hurried to join her brother, and they headed into the emergency room for a brief visit with their father.

* * *

Jacob waited with Annie and Josiah while Horseshoe Joe was in surgery. He could tell that Annie was anxious. Josiah was quiet and didn't have much to say. Within the hour, Nancy King arrived, greeted them and then sat next to Josiah. Annie's brother's expression brightened; he was obviously glad to see her.

Jacob glanced at the couple, then averted his gaze. Nancy had been *his* sweetheart, if only for a short time. They had parted ways after she'd gone with her grandparents to visit relatives in North Carolina. On her return, something was changed between them. It was almost as if they'd never spent time together. And then Nancy had begun walking out with Josiah.

He'd felt hurt at the time, but later when he'd thought about it, he realized that he hadn't been too upset by the breakup. God had helped him understand that Nancy King wasn't the woman he was intended to marry. If he'd loved Nancy as much as Noah loved Rachel or Jed loved Sarah, he might have tried to win Nancy's affection again. But he hadn't; he'd simply accepted that their relationship was over.

Thinking about marriage, Jacob knew that he had nothing to offer a wife. If Nancy hadn't gone away, he might have married her, but he didn't know how he would have provided for her, or for any woman he courted with the intention of marrying. He was getting older now and had to think about his future.

"Jacob?" Annie interrupted his thoughts. "Dr. Moss warned us that this would be a long surgery. It will be another hour, at least, until *Dat* is in recovery."

"I'll wait," he said. She hadn't always been a prickly thing. Her breakup with his eldest brother Jedidiah must have changed her.

Annie stood, and he followed suit.

"Restless?" he asked her.

She nodded. "It's going to be a long while yet."

"Let's go downstairs for coffee," he said, expecting her to refuse. She surprised him when she agreed.

"Josiah, we are going down to the cafeteria for coffee," Annie said. "Would you like to come?"

"*Nay.* I'll stay," her brother said, and Nancy edged closer to him. His expression softened. "If we hear anything," he told his sister, "we'll let you know." He had taken off his hat and he held it between his knees, twirling the brim.

Jacob saw that Josiah was more upset than he'd originally let on. "This is an awful thing, but the Lord will help your *vadder.*"

Josiah stared at him a second and then gave a nod. "*Ja.* When you are done," he asked, "would you bring up coffee for us?"

"*Ja,*" Jacob said with a slight smile. "We won't be long." He knew Annie would want to return as soon as they'd entered the cafeteria. She wouldn't be able to help it; he could tell she was terrified that something awful would happen to her father during surgery.

He followed her into the elevator, pushed the button and stood silently, studying her as he waited for them to reach the bottom floor. She didn't look at him once during the entire ride. It didn't bode well for their having coffee together. He would just have to somehow put her at ease.

Chapter Two

Jacob studied Annie across the table as she sipped from her cup of coffee, set the mug down and stared into its contents. The hospital cafeteria was quiet. The long institutional-type tables were empty except for Annie and him and two female nurses and a male hospital worker, who occupied another table on the other side of the room. It was too late for breakfast and too early for lunch. "How's the coffee?" he asked softly.

She lifted her gaze from the steaming mug. *"Gut."* He could see the sheen from the rising moisture on her forehead. She looked at him a moment, her blue eyes shimmering with unshed tears, then glanced away. He could see how the events of the morning had taken a toll on her. "Jacob, I appreciate your help with *Dat*," she said, almost reluctantly.

"I didn't do much—"

"I don't know what I would have done if you hadn't stopped to help," she admitted.

"I wouldn't have left you," he assured her. "I knew something was wrong the minute I saw you." He frowned. "How are your feet?"

She blushed as she shifted briefly to glance beneath

the table at her grandmother's navy sneakers, worn over her grandfather's black socks. "They are fine. They barely hurt."

"Must have been broken glass alongside the road."

"I was so scared, I just ran," she admitted. "I didn't take time to look down." Her blond hair was a beautiful shade of gold beneath her white head covering. After the blush of embarrassment left her, she looked pale, too pale.

"May I get you something to eat?" he asked. She looked lovely and vulnerable; he wished he could do more for her.

Annie shook her head. "I'm not hungry."

"We've been here for over two hours and the only thing you've had is that coffee. Once your *vadder* is out of surgery, you may not have another opportunity to eat. How about a sandwich?" When she declined, he said, "A cookie? A piece of cake?"

She didn't answer. He heard her sniff. "Annie." Jacob hated to see her troubled, but he understood. *"Annie."*

She looked up, started to rise. "We should get back."

He stood. "I'll get the coffee for Josiah and Nancy. You can go ahead if you'd like."

She shook her head. *"Nay* I'll wait for you," she said, surprising him. "You may need help with the coffee."

Jacob paid for the drinks for Josiah and Nancy, and on impulse, he purchased two large chocolate-chip cookies. He tucked them under the coffee fixings in the center of the cardboard cup holder. He was back with Annie in less than a minute. There'd been no one in line at the register. "I grabbed sugar and cream for the coffee," he told her. She inclined her head.

He silently rode with her on the elevator up to the surgical floor. The doors opened and Jacob waited for Annie to precede him. To his surprise, she suddenly stopped and turned to him. "What are we going to do, Jacob? How will we make do, when *Dat* can't work?"

Jacob considered the woman before him, noting the concern in her expression. "I can help out in the shop, and our community will be there for you, too."

She shook her head. "You don't have enough experience. You could do more harm than good."

"I'm not a boy, Annie. I can do the job." There was a charged moment as awareness of her sprung up inside him. Jacob shook it off. "If I don't do it, who will?"

"I don't know." She seemed to think about it. "I'll have to ask *Dat*."

She had grabbed his hat from the table, where he'd set it down when he'd gone for the coffee for her brother and Nancy. Now she fingered the brim nervously.

"We are friends, aren't we, Annie?" he asked. "I remember seeing you in the open shop doorway when we were *kinner*, watching me with your *dat*."

She hesitated, then smiled slightly. "I was sure you would burn yourself with the hot metal, but you never did."

"Not that you ever saw." He remembered her as a young girl, the first girl he'd ever liked.

Her expression turned serious. "Jacob, it's nice of you to offer your help, but we can't accept it."

"But if Joe agrees?" he said softly.

"Then I guess the decision will be made." She continued down the hall toward the surgical waiting room.

Jacob fell into step beside her. He studied her bent head, admiring the beauty of her profile. She looked pale and tense, and he didn't seem to be able to help. He saw Josiah leave the waiting room up ahead and approach.

"How's *Dat*?" Annie asked.

"No word yet from the doctor." Josiah nodded his

thanks as Jacob handed him a cup of coffee. He declined sugar and cream and grabbed the other cup for Nancy.

Inside the waiting room, Jacob set down the cardboard cup holder, accepted his hat back from Annie and then took a seat near her. They waited in silence. He retrieved and handed her the wrapped cookies. "For when you're hungry."

Annie's eyes locked with his. She opened her mouth to say something but then nodded silently instead. Jacob found that he couldn't look away.

"Are those cookies?" Josiah asked, capturing Annie's attention.

"*Ja*, Jacob bought them." Annie handed him one, and Josiah beamed.

"*Gut* thinking, Jacob," Josiah said before he unwrapped the treat and broke it in half. He handed a piece to Nancy and then took a bite of his own.

Jacob smiled. He was pleased to see Josiah enjoying it, even more pleased to note that Annie had kept one for herself.

It wasn't long before there was a light commotion right outside the waiting room. Soon, others within their Amish community arrived, having received word of Joe's accident. As the newcomers entered the room, he got up and moved away to give Josiah and Annie the time to be comforted by their friends. Among the new arrivals were his parents—Katie and Samuel Lapp—Josie and William Mast and Mae and Amos King. Annie and Josiah rose, and their friends immediately surrounded them.

William Mast took off his hat, held it against his chest. "How's Joe?" he asked Jacob.

Jacob acknowledged the older man. "He's still in surgery."

"Any idea how long?" the older bearded man asked.

When Jacob explained it could be another half hour or more, William left to stand near his wife, Josie, who was comforting Annie.

Josie moved aside, and Jacob's mother stepped in to give Annie a hug. She spoke briefly to her and Josiah before she moved back to allow others to talk with the Zook siblings.

His *mam* turned and saw him standing outside the group. She approached. "How bad?"

"Bad enough." Jacob was conscious of Annie across the room. He glanced over briefly to see how she was faring, before he turned back to his mother.

"Isaac stopped by the house to tell us," *Mam* told him. "You never know what can happen." She touched his arm. "What was he doing on the roof?"

"Trying to repair a leak."

"Why didn't he ask for help? Joe knows your *dat* or one of you boys would have done the work."

"Perhaps he wanted to do it himself." Jacob held out his coffee toward her. "Would you like a sip?" After his mother declined, he drank from the cup, grimaced, then walked toward a trash can and dropped the remainder inside. "Good choice," he told her with a grin.

"Jed would have come, but he's working construction today and there was no way to reach him." *Mam* glanced briefly toward the Zook siblings. "Sarah stayed at the house with Hannah. And Noah—"

Jacob nodded. He knew exactly why Noah hadn't come. He was worried about leaving his wife, Rachel, who had lost their baby a month before her due date. Even now, months later, while she appeared strong to the outside world, Noah continually fretted about her.

The double doors leading to the surgical area swung

open and Dr. Moss, dressed in green medical scrubs, stepped out and approached Annie and Josiah.

Jacob worried about Annie as she moved to stand next to her brother so Dr. Moss could inform them of the outcome of her father's surgery. Nancy King stood on Josiah's other side. He saw Josiah reach out to clasp hands with both women. Dr. Moss spoke at length, but from where he was, Jacob couldn't hear. He stepped closer.

"The surgery went well," the doctor said. "Your father is in recovery now. You'll be able to go back and see him for a few minutes, but don't be alarmed if he doesn't respond. It will take him a while to come out of the anesthesia…"

Jacob saw Mae King slip an arm around Annie, watched as Annie leaned into the older woman for a moment's comfort before she straightened. Her eyes narrowed as she looked about. Her glance slid over him without pausing before it moved on.

They'll take care of her, he thought as he studied the group who were doing their best to be there for Joe's children. Annie didn't need him now. It was time for him to leave, to see what needed to be done at the Zook farm while Annie and Josiah stayed close to their father.

"I'm going to head back," he told his parents as his father joined them.

His mother studied him, gave him a slight smile. "We'll stay for a while."

"You have a ride?" his father asked.

"Bob Whittier." Jacob glanced at the clock, noted the time. "He should be here soon."

Samuel nodded. "Are you going home?"

"Nay," Jacob said. "I thought I'd go to the Zooks' farm first."

* * *

Rick Martin pulled into the Zook barnyard late that afternoon to drop off Annie and Josiah. He promised to return the next morning to take them back to the hospital. After Rick had left, Josiah sighed and ran a hand along the back of his neck. "I'll check on the animals."

Annie watched him walk away. "Are you hungry?" she called. "I can fix us something."

He stopped and turned. *"Ja,"* he admitted. "Anything will do."

As her brother walked to the barn, Annie headed toward the farmhouse. She froze in her tracks. *Millie,* she thought with alarm. Where was Millie? In all the commotion, she'd forgotten to put her dog back into the house before leaving for the hospital.

"Josiah!" she called. "Please watch for Millie. She got out of the house earlier."

Josiah scowled but agreed. "She'll come back eventually."

Annie opened the screen door and the inside door swung open. It didn't surprise her that she hadn't locked it after she'd grabbed her purse. Her one thought had been to get to her father.

She entered the house and wandered into the gathering room. Annie stiffened at what she saw. All of the laundry was stacked, neatly folded, inside the laundry basket. She experienced a chill. Someone had been here. *But a burglar wouldn't fold laundry,* she thought.

She heard a short bark and was startled when Millie scurried into the room, wagging her tail happily. Annie bent down to rub her beloved pet's fur. "How did you get in here?"

"Annie," a deep voice said.

She gasped and spun toward the man who'd entered

from the direction of the kitchen. *"Jacob?"* She rose to her feet, stared at him. "What are you doing here?"

"Sorry." His golden eyes studied her with concern. "I didn't mean to frighten you. I stopped by to look for Millie and found her. I suddenly remembered her running about before we left."

"You shouldn't have come." She peered up at him with caution. "You folded the laundry." Why would he fold laundry? The men in her Amish community didn't fold laundry! It was an unheard of thing for any man to help with women's work. "Why?"

He shrugged. "You didn't get the chance, so I thought I'd finish it for you." He flashed a brief glance at the clothes before refocusing on her.

Her spine tingled. "I could have done it."

His lips curved with amusement. "I don't doubt it."

Millie licked her leg, demanding her attention. "You found Millie."

"I found her chasing a cat through the fields." He traced the edge of his suspenders with his fingers. "The door was open, so I brought her in."

Watching, Annie wondered why her heart suddenly began to beat faster. "I forgot to lock the door."

"Not to worry. No one disturbed the house." Jacob was suddenly there beside her.

Overwhelmed by his nearness, she stepped back. "No one but you," she accused.

She heard him sigh. "You look like you're about to collapse," he said quietly. "Come. You've had a terrible day. Sit and I'll make you some hot tea."

She sat down. "I can make my own tea."

"Ja, I'm sure you can." He narrowed his eyes at her from above. "But I'd like to make you a cup. Is that a problem?"

Feeling foolish, Annie shook her head. Reaction to *Dat's* accident took over and suddenly cold she started to shake. She looked at him, but she couldn't seem to focus. She felt warmth override the chill and realized that Jacob had grabbed the quilt from her father's favorite chair and gently placed it around her shoulders. With mixed feelings, she watched him leave the room. He wasn't gone long.

"Here you go." Jacob held her hot tea. The sofa cushion dipped beneath her as he sat beside her. He extended the cup, and when she didn't immediately respond, gently placed it within her hands, his strong fingers cradling hers until she became overly conscious of his touch.

She realized what he was doing, and she jerked back. "I've got it," she said, relieved that he'd let go and that she hadn't spilled any. He stood, and Annie felt the heat from the mug. She raised the rim to her lips.

"Careful!" he warned. "It's hot." He seemed upset as his golden eyes regarded her apologetically. "I shouldn't have let it boil."

"It's fine, Jacob," she said irritably. "If the water isn't hot, it's not a *gut* cup of tea." Annie took a tentative drink. The steaming brew was sweet. She felt revived after several slow, tiny sips. She looked up at him. *"Danki,"* she said when she felt more like herself again.

Jacob gave her a slow smile that did odd things to her insides. She fought back those feelings. He studied her a long moment until he was apparently satisfied with what he saw. "Did you see your *vadder*?" His voice was soft as he moved the laundry basket from the sofa to the floor and sat down.

Taken aback by her reaction to him, Annie fought to stay calm. *"Ja*, we saw him. Once he was in his hospital room. When he finally woke up, he told us he was tired and wanted us to go home." She drew a deep breath. "Jacob, I'm fine, You don't have to stay—"

He nodded. "Where's Josiah?"

"In the barn."

"I took care of the animals earlier," he said.

The front door slammed. "Annie," Josiah called out, "the animals have been fed and watered—"

Annie met his gaze as her brother entered the room and stopped abruptly. "Jacob took care of them."

Jacob rose to his feet. He and Josiah stared at one another a long moment, and Annie remembered suddenly that Nancy King, the girl Jacob had fancied and lost, was currently her brother's sweetheart.

"I appreciate what you did for *Dat*." Josiah extended his hand.

She watched the interaction between the two men and then saw Jacob smile. They shook hands and stepped back.

"I should go," Jacob said. Annie watched him grab his hat off a wall hook. "You both need your rest." He hesitated. "I made sandwiches. I put them in the refrigerator."

Annie blinked, shocked. "You made yourself at home."

He raised an eyebrow at her tone. "*Nay*. I simply fixed a meal for friends in need." He jammed his hat on his head. He gave a nod to her brother. "Josiah."

"Jacob." Josiah inclined his head.

As Jacob headed outside, Annie felt as if she'd been too mean-spirited toward him, and it didn't set well with her. It wasn't the way of her community or the Lord— and it wasn't like her to behave this way, either.

Annie followed him, stopping to stand in the open doorway as he descended the porch steps. "*Gut* day to *you*, Jacob Lapp," she called out to him.

He paused and turned. "Rest well, Annie Zook," he replied and then he walked away, without glancing back.

Annie felt awful as she watched him leave. Contrary to her behavior, she had appreciated having Jacob nearby. His quiet strength and presence had soothed her during the crisis with her *dat*. She reminded herself that he was her childhood friend, and she shouldn't worry about spending time with him. He wasn't Jed, and he wasn't in the position to break her heart.

Chapter Three

"Aren't you done with that family?"

Jacob buttoned his light blue shirt without glancing toward his twin brother. "Which family?"

"The Zooks." The mattress springs squeaked as Eli sat and kicked against the bed's wooden frame.

"What are *you* trying to tell me?" He knew what Eli was hinting at, but he wanted to hear him say it.

"I'm reminding you that while Horseshoe Joe was *gut* to you, you can't say the same for his daughter."

Jacob sighed as he pulled one suspender over his shoulder before drawing up the other one. "So, I once liked Annie, and she liked Jed. I got over her years ago."

"So you say." Eli rose from his bed, bent to pick up a shoe, which he pointed at Jacob. "Mark my words. She still pines for him, Jake. Even though he's married to Sarah now."

Jacob grabbed the black shoe, and with a teasing look Eli retrieved the other one from the floor for him. "And I shouldn't help Horseshoe Joe because Annie likes Jed?" He snatched the second shoe from Eli's hand and set both back onto the floor. He pulled on his socks.

"Nay," Eli said. "I just want you to be mindful of the

past. I know *ya* like the back of my own hand, like you know me." He grinned, and his blue eyes crinkled at the corners. "We are twins after all." He plucked a straw hat off the wall peg.

"We are?" Jacob replied with feigned surprise. He grinned as he snatched his hat from his twin's hands and tossed it on the bed. "I'm not a boy, Eli. Neither are you. And I'm not pining for Annie." Although he was very glad he'd been able to help in her time of need. "Do you ever think about marrying someday?"

"Ja, I think about it." Eli ran a hand through his golden-blond hair. "But until I find the right one to wed, I'll not be thinking too much of it." He grinned, displaying even white teeth.

Jacob laughed. He loved his brother, not necessarily more than the rest but differently, with the love born of brothers who'd entered this earth on the same day. *A relationship which started in* Mam's *womb*, he thought. The connection between them was strong. They'd been raised from the cradle together, although no one looking at them would believe them twins. Eli's hair was as fair as his was dark. Day and night, someone had once said of them. They might be different in looks, but that was all. They were close, often sharing each other's thoughts, sometimes finishing each other's sentences.

Eli, more than anyone, had understood how he'd felt when Annie Zook had finally won Jed's attention. They'd been sixteen years old, and although it had been years since he'd stopped hanging about Zook's Blacksmithy, hoping for a glimpse of Annie, his loss hadn't been any less painful. He was over Annie, and she certainly didn't care for him. So why was she so wary of him? Simply because Jed was his brother?

"You don't have to worry about me." Jacob slipped on

his shoes, then propped a foot onto a wooden chest to tie his shoelaces. "Annie made it clear that she only tolerates me because I stopped to help Joe. Once the ambulance arrived, she wanted me to leave." He lowered his right leg and raised his left.

"But you stayed anyway," Eli pointed out.

"Ja." Jacob finished up and straightened. "I went to the hospital *and* the *haus*." When he'd returned home the day of Horseshoe Joe's accident, he had confided in Eli how he'd gone to the Zooks' to check on the house and Millie, and dared to stay to help out. Annie hadn't liked it, although she'd seemed grateful that he'd found her dog. "Why should I care what she thinks? I was concerned about Joe. And I was worried about her dog."

Eli laughed. "You were worried about the dog." His brother regarded him with sympathy, as if Jacob were fooling himself to think that his time at Annie's had anything to do with an animal. "And now you're going to talk with Horseshoe Joe, to see if he'll let you take over his work in his shop until he is well. From what I've heard, his recovery could take twelve weeks or more." Eli paused. "That's a long time.

"Ja, I know, but I'll be available if *Dat* needs me." He retrieved his hat from the bed, then preceded Eli out of their room and down the stairs to the first floor. "If I have to, I'll work part-time in the shop and the rest at the farm."

"As long as Horseshoe Joe agrees," Eli said from behind him.

"As long as Joe agrees to what?" Isaac asked as he came out from the back of the house.

"Jacob is going to offer to work in the blacksmith shop while Joe recovers," Eli told their younger brother.

Isaac shrugged as he continued past them. "I'm sure

Joe will appreciate it," he threw back over his shoulder, before he started up the stairs.

"Jake, I hope you know what you're doing." Eli followed his brother into the yard. "Helping Joe will put you in frequent company with Annie.

"It will," Jacob said. "And her sister Barbara. Shall I worry about her, too?"

Eli chuckled. "Maybe you should."

"Jacob!" *Dat* exited the house and approached. "Heading over to the Zooks'?" Jacob nodded. "I'd like to go with you."

"I'll bring around the buggy." Jacob flashed a cheeky glance at his twin brother before he headed toward the family's gray buggy, parked near the barn. As he climbed into the vehicle and grabbed up the leathers, he thought of what his brother had said, and he knew that Eli was right. He had liked Annie Zook as a boy, and she had liked—still liked—his brother Jed. But he was no longer a boy. He was a man who could control his emotions. Besides, without any means to offer a wife, he'd not be thinking of courting or marrying anytime in the near future.

"When are you going to think about marrying?"

Annie looked up from the piecrust she'd been rolling on a floured board on the kitchen worktable. "*Mam*, who said I don't think about it?"

Her mother went to a cabinet and withdrew a tin of cinnamon. "I don't mean about marrying Jedidiah Lapp. That one is taken. It's time you looked elsewhere."

"I know that." She set down the wooden rolling pin and then wiped her hands on a tea towel. "It's not as if I can marry the next man who walks through that door," Annie said patiently as she carefully lifted the edge of the crust and set it into the pie pan. With skill born of experience, she molded the dough against the sides and then turned under the excess along the rim before she pressed the edges into place with a dinner fork.

Mam set the cinnamon tin within her reach and then began to cut up a stick of butter. "Annie," she said softly. "I know Jed hurt you, and I understand that you've decided it would be better for you to marry someone older—"

"*Much* older," Annie said with a smile for her mother. "A man who will care for me and accept me as I am. It's a *gut* plan."

"Maybe," *Mam* said, nodding. "I don't know that you should limit your choices. You're not getting any younger."

"*Mam!*" Annie began to core and cut up fresh cooking apples.

"'Tis true." *Mam* started to help her, grabbing an apple and slicing it in half. "The thing is, Annie, your *vadder's* accident is going to hurt us financially. I have faith that his hospital bills will be paid, but with him unable to work in the shop…"

Annie recalled Jacob Lapp's offer to help, then she promptly forced it from her mind. Jacob had apparently taken her at her word that he couldn't fill in for *Dat*, and that was fine. "What does *Dat's* accident have to do with me marrying?"

Mam had cut up two apples, and she reached for a third. "We'd like to see you settled with a husband, someone who can provide for you."

She felt the blood drain from her face. "You and *Dat* want me to wed so that you don't have to provide for me?"

"*Nay*," *Mam* said, "that's not what I'm saying at all. Your *dat* and I love you. But we—I—worry that you've not considered your future. You're a caring young woman. You'll make some man a fine wife."

"I'll not approach a man and ask him to marry me," Annie said, horrified at the idea.

"Nay." *Mam* dumped the apples into a large bowl, which she pushed toward Annie. "I'm simply saying that if a man shows interest in you, you consider him seriously."

Annie sprinkled sugar and cinnamon over the apples and stirred them through. "I will," she said, "if one shows interest." She didn't have much to worry about. No man since Jed Lapp had taken notice of her yet.

Mam smiled. *"Gut.* I like having you here—it's not that."

She felt herself relax. "I know you want only what's best for me."

"Ja," *Mam* said. "I want what's best for all of my children."

The thud of footsteps resounded on the front wooden porch—the new covered porch with the wheelchair ramp, built by the church community men to help with her father's recovery.

"Miriam?" Samuel Lapp's voice called out as he approached the screen door.

Annie smiled as her mother left the kitchen to greet Samuel. She liked Jedidiah Lapp's *dat.* He was a kind, caring man, who loved his family and was always available for whenever anyone within their church community needed him. As she continued to work on the apple pie, she heard murmuring voices. Samuel must have come to visit with her father. She carefully spooned the apples onto the crust, aware of when her mother entered the kitchen. *"Mam,* would you pass me the container of brown sugar? I left it on the counter."

The container of brown sugar was set before her. She looked up to smile her thanks and then promptly froze at the sight of Jacob Lapp, standing on the other side of the table, watching her with his laughing, golden eyes.

"What are you doing here?" she snapped. His dark hair looked neatly combed despite the fact that he had obviously just removed his hat upon entering the house. His jaw was clean shaven, like all of the other unmarried young men within their village of Happiness. She lifted her gaze from the smooth skin of his chin and cheeks to a nose that was well formed and masculine, up to those twinkling tawny eyes of his. It felt like dancing butterflies flitted across her nape as some unknown emotion passed over her. Disturbed, she quickly looked away.

"Your *mudder* sent me for the pitcher of iced tea. *Dat* and I have come for a visit with your *vadder*."

Her heart raced as she narrowed her eyes at him. "The tea is over there," she instructed, "in the refrigerator." She gestured toward a back room. Aware of her flour- and cinnamon-dusted hands, she quickly went back to work, fixing the crumb topping that would form the upper "crust" of the apple pie. She was aware that Jacob hadn't moved. She could feel him studying her and pretended she didn't notice until her mother returned from the family gathering room, where her father spent the better part of his days recuperating.

"Did you find the iced tea, Jacob?" *Mam* asked.

"Annie just told me where to find it," he said.

"I'll get it," her mother offered as Jacob moved closer to the worktable.

He leaned forward, nearly invading her space. She stepped back and glared at him. He simply smiled at her. "That looks *gut*," he said. "I always enjoy being in the kitchen on *Mam's* baking day."

Annie paused, looked up. "Making an apple pie?" she taunted.

A slow smile curved his handsome lips. "I don't cook, but I've helped a time or two." Her mother returned from the back room and handed him the iced tea. He held on to the glass pitcher and said, "Nothing like a slice of hot apple pie, fresh from the oven on baking day."

"Except maybe a piece of warm apple pie with a scoop of homemade ice cream." *Mam* went to the pantry and took out a tray of cookies. "Pie won't be done for a while, how about these instead?"

"These are great." Jacob grinned, and Annie told herself that she wasn't affected by his smile or his good looks.

"Annie made them," *Mam* said, and Annie wanted to cry out with frustration.

"You helped." She measured out the brown sugar, dumped it in a small bowl and added the butter her mother had cut up earlier.

Jacob grabbed a chocolate-chip cookie from the plate and took a bite. "Delicious."

Annie shot him a glance and felt her heart flutter at his look. "It's just a cookie," she said, her tone sharp. *There is no need to be hostile*, she reminded herself. She drew a calming breath and managed to smile. "I'm glad you like it."

Why was he here? Why did he seek her out? Had Jed said something to him about her? She didn't want to know, for she feared the truth might hurt her.

"I'll take these into the other room." Jacob sniffed, as if detecting a scent. "I can smell them. Lemon?" He took another whiff and nodded. "And this one here smells like almond extract." He held up the plate with one hand. "I'd sure like to try that pie."

Annie saw Jacob smile at her mother, felt the bright light of it and looked away. She was relieved when he left the room with the refreshments, for she didn't want to notice anything about him—or to remember the attractive, teasing twinkle in his eyes while he ate one of her cookies.

"Jacob!" Horseshoe Joe sat in his chair with his leg cast propped up on a padded stool that Jacob's brother Noah had made for him.

"We were just talking about you," Samuel said.

Jacob raised his eyebrows as he approached with iced tea and cookies and set them down. "What about?"

"Joe wants to ask you something," his father said.

He glanced back and forth between the two older men. *"Ja?"* He was pleased to note that Joe looked much better since his return home nearly two weeks before. The color had returned to the older man's cheeks. But Joe couldn't get around well yet.

Joe tried to adjust his leg, and Jacob's *dat* helped him shift it to a more comfortable position. "You must know that I still have weeks of recovery before me." Jacob nodded. "I go back to the doctor next Tuesday." The older man suddenly seemed uncertain. "I was wondering, Jake…"

Concerned, Jacob placed a hand on his shoulder. "What is it, Joe?"

"Would *ya* consider taking over for me until I'm well?" Joe asked quickly. Seated next to him in a wooden chair, Jacob's father was nodding.

Jacob stepped back. "You want me to take over your work in the shop?" He thought of Annie. Maybe he shouldn't accept the job. He didn't want to antagonize the woman further, if he could help it. But how could he deny Joe his assistance, especially since the thought of returning to the art of blacksmithing tempted him?

Joe nodded. "If you would. I know you're busy, but you would be a big help, if you could. If not, I'll understand." He reached up to rub his bearded chin. "I'll pay you for your work."

"*Nay*, if I do this, you'll not be paying me." Jacob picked up the cookies, placed them within Joe's reach and then chose to sit across the room. He suffered a moment of doubt but couldn't ignore the expectant look on Horseshoe Joe's face. He sighed inwardly. Annie wouldn't like it, but he had to help out Joe. "I'll be more than happy to help *you*, Joe." While the idea of working in the shop thrilled him, it also gave him a little chill. "It's been years since I helped—bothered—you with my interest in blacksmithing. I was only a boy."

"At twelve, you were hardly a boy. You have a talent for the job, son. I had faith in you then, and I have faith that you can do the work now." He grinned. "And I'll be nearby if *ya* happen to need me."

"Josiah doesn't want to step in?"

Joe shook his head. "He never learned about forging metal, never wanted to. You are the only one who took an interest in my work and my business. You and my girls, Annie and Barbara, who liked to watch when they were younger."

"And I liked to be in the thick of everything," Jacob agreed.

"*Ja*, you did." Joe exchanged glances with Jacob's father.

"Will *you* do it, Jake?" his father asked.

"Heat and bend metal, watch it glow?" Jacob grinned. "*Ja*, I'll do it."

"Do what?" Annie asked as she entered the room with

clear glasses. She set them down, picked up the pitcher and began to pour out the tea.

"Jacob's agreed to fill in for me at the shop," Joe said.

"That's nice of him," Annie said after a lengthy pause. When she shot him an angry glance, Jacob raised an eyebrow at her.

He noted a bit of flour dust on her cheek and in her hair. She wore a patchwork apron over a spring-green dress. A few strands of her blond hair had escaped from the edge of her prayer *kapp*, where she must have wiped cinnamon from her forehead with the back of her hand. The cinnamon was still there—barely. He could detect the scent rather than see any of the spice's warm brown color.

As she worked to fill each glass, he watched emotion play across her features. It moved so fast no one else might have noticed, but he did. She wasn't happy that he'd be coming to the farm daily. She hadn't known about her father's plan. Jacob felt a smile start, but he stifled it until she briefly looked his way, and then he released it.

"That will be a great help to *Dat*," she said, turning away, and his amusement grew.

"*Ja*, I'll be around to help every day—" he glanced toward Joe "—or whenever *ya* need me to come."

"Can you start tomorrow?" Joe asked.

Jacob looked to his father. "Can you make do without me on the farm?"

His *dat* nodded. "I've plenty of help." He turned toward his friend. "Tomorrow will be fine, Joe."

"Then I'll be here then." Jacob watched Joe reach for a cookie. Recalling his enjoyment of his first one, he reached for another. Annie Zook was a fine baker. He flashed Annie an admiring glance as she turned to stare at him, before she looked away. He continued to study her. For some reason, she always found fault with him. He didn't know what bothered her about him, but he was sure he'd find out eventually. For now, he had to concentrate on doing a good job at Zook's Blacksmithy. "I'll not let you down, Joe," he said.

Horseshoe Joe swallowed before answering. "Never thought *ya* would." He grinned as he brought the cookie to his lips. "I know you'll do me proud," he said before taking another bite.

"If not," *Dat* said, "he'll have to answer to me." His teasing tone made Jacob smile.

"It's not you I worry about, *Dat*."

"*Nay*, it's your *mudder*." And the three men laughed together at his father's remark, while Annie scurried out of the room.

Chapter Four

Jacob stood in the center of Zook's Blacksmithy and examined the shop. He felt a little nervous pull in his gut. Could he do this and do it well? His attention focused on the tools hanging on the wall: metal tongs, cross-peen hammers and other various tools for shaping metal, before it moved to the steel anvil not far from the brick forge.

You must be careful you don't burn yourself, Jacob, Joe had warned him time and again when he was a boy. *Hold these tongs just so—* The man had shown him how to use the tool. *These will get hot, as well.* He had gestured toward his leather apron. *This garment protects my clothes from sparks and heat.*

One particular day after Jacob, as a young boy, had been coming to the shop for weeks, Joe had pulled out a slightly smaller version of his leather apron and handed it to him. Jacob had accepted the garment with wide eyes, pleased that Joe trusted him enough to let him try his hand at blacksmithing.

The memory of Joe's patient voice calmed him. Suddenly, everything within the shop seemed familiar again.

He just had to remember all the things that Joe had taught him, and he'd do fine.

"Jacob."

Startled, Jacob spun, surprised to see Joe in his wheelchair. Annie stood behind him in the open doorway, looking beautiful in a light blue dress, black apron and with a white prayer *kapp* on her golden-blond hair. She appeared concerned for her father. In direct contrast, Horseshoe Joe looked pale beneath his white-streaked brown beard. He had left his hat in the house, and his tousled graying hair made him look much older than his forty-some years. "Joe, *ya* shouldn't be here. You should be resting and recovering."

Joe nodded. "I just wanted to check in on your first day here. Is there anything you need? Anything you want to know?"

The memory of Joe's teachings gave Jacob the confidence to smile. "I remember everything you taught me. I'll be fine."

"I never doubted that," Joe replied. "You make sure you stop a time or two and come to the house for something to eat."

"If I get hungry, I will," Jacob said. He smiled at Annie. She glanced quickly away and he turned his attention back to Horseshoe Joe. "Do you have a list of any back orders?" he asked.

"Ja," Joe said. "Annie, push me closer." He gestured toward the other side of the shop.

"Dat..."

"I'm not going to work, daughter. I'm hardly in a position to do anything but sit—and even that's getting painful." Annie pushed her father's wheelchair farther into the room. "This is fine, Annie." Joe gestured toward a wall shelf. "Jacob? See that notebook? Inside, you'll find a list of special orders. Not horseshoes but cabinet hinges, tools for specific use and other requests."

Jacob pulled the book from its nesting place on the shelf. He flipped through pages, seeing Joe's notes. "This will be helpful."

Joe looked tired. "There will be the usual orders for horseshoes. Abram Peachy has been patiently waiting for me to shoe one of his mares. If you can take care of that soon, I'd appreciate it." Jacob saw a hint of tears in the older man's eyes. "*Danki*, Jacob."

"I'm grateful you had the patience to teach me about blacksmithing when I was younger," Jacob replied.

"I enjoyed having you in the shop, interested in my work." Joe smiled.

Jacob grinned. His good humor dimmed as he met Annie's gaze briefly before returning his attention to her father. "Go home and rest. Things will be fine here."

Joe's smile was weak. "I think I'll do that."

"It was *gut* of you to visit me on my first day," Jacob said. He gave Annie a nod, and she acknowledged it politely. He knew that she would take good care of her father.

As she pushed Joe from the shop, Jacob sighed. *Annie.* He had a lot to do and he didn't need his thoughts muddled with Annie Zook and whether or not she approved of him. A blacksmith's job took concentration, skill and patience, and he planned to ensure that Zook's Blacksmithy continued to run smoothly in Horseshoe Joe's absence.

Annie pushed her father up the wheelchair ramp and into the house. "You'll be resting now, *Dat*?"

Her father sighed. "*Ja.* I'm feeling weak."

"'Tis to be expected. You've done too much today." She eyed him with concern. "Is your shin hurting?"

He nodded. "I'll just sit in my chair and put up my leg."

"Do *ya* need a pain pill?"

"*Nay*. I'll be fine. Would you get me a cup of tea?"

Annie smiled. "I'll bring you some of your favorite cookies, too." She helped him move to his favorite chair. With Annie's help, he set both of his legs onto the stool Noah Lapp had made for him and closed his eyes.

Annie picked up a quilt, spread it carefully over his legs and tucked it in near his waist. "I'll be right back, *Dat.*"

He acknowledged her with a small sound that told her he might be ready to sleep. Still, she left the room and entered the kitchen to put on a pot of tea. As she placed the kettle on the stove, she thought of Jacob. It was strange to see him in the shop again. Watching him take stock of Zook's Blacksmithy, she became overly conscious that he was no longer a boy but an attractive man.

I'm older and wiser; I won't make the same mistake twice. She wouldn't fall for another Lapp brother.

When the water was hot, she poured it into a teapot and added two bags. She'd enjoy a cup, too. Her mother and sister were not home; they were next door at her *grosseldre's* house.

When the tea had steeped, she poured out two cups. After filling a plate with treats, she went back to the gathering room and her father. Her *dat* opened his eyes when she entered the room.

"*Gut,*" he said. "Those cookies look delicious." He smiled when Annie placed his tea just the way he liked it on the table beside him.

"I put more than one kind on the plate," she said as she offered him a napkin and extended the dish.

"They're all my favorite," he said with a weak grin.

There was a tired look about his eyes, but there was enjoyment, too. Annie was happy to see it. "Annie." Her father captured her hand as she turned to leave. "Take the boy something to eat later."

Annie frowned. "Boy?"

"Jacob," *Dat* said as he took a bite.

"Jacob's not a boy, *Dat*." She held out the plate for him.

"Man, then," her father corrected as he selected another cookie.

She opened her mouth to say more but promptly thought better of it. "I'll make him something to eat."

"How about that leftover chicken potpie of yours?"

"*Mam* made it." She rubbed her nape with her left hand. "I'll bring him a bowlful and something to drink."

"*Nay*, Annie. Invite him to eat lunch with us," her *dat* said. "He's doing me a favor by pitching in."

"Are *ya* sure he'll do a *gut* enough job for you?" she asked. She was upset that Jacob hadn't waited for her to talk with her father about the idea.

"He'll do a fine job." *Dat* took a sip of his tea. "I taught him well."

"But he was only eleven or twelve then," she said. "That was a long time ago."

"He's a natural. He hasn't forgotten what to do." Her father smiled. "Shouldn't your *mudder* be back by now?"

Annie shook her head. "She and Barbara are cleaning for *Grossmudder*."

"And you had *vadder* duty," *Dat* said sadly.

She settled her hand on his shoulder. "*Dat*, 'tis my pleasure to be here for you."

Her father regarded her with affection. "I know."

Annie saw her *dat's* eyes brighten as he caught sight of her dog, Millie, curled up in her bed. He'd grown attached to the dog since his accident.

"Millie," she called softly. The dog picked up her head. "Go sit by *Dat*." As if she understood, little Millie rose from her bed and went to lie next to the base of Joe's chair. "Watch him for me, girl."

"Bring Jacob some water when you ask him to lunch. Working in the shop makes a man thirsty," Joe said as he closed his eyes.

Annie stiffened. *"Ja, Dat,"* she said dutifully. In the kitchen, she filled a large plastic jug with water. She then grabbed a cup and a plate of cookies before she reluctantly headed out to the barn.

Jacob pulled out the tools he needed to make the horseshoes for Abram Peachy's mare and stoked up the fire in the forge. He could use the propane torch but not today. He wanted to do it the way he'd first been taught. The leather apron Joe had bought for him still hung in the shop, as if it were only a day rather than years since he'd visited last. Jacob fingered the material. It was too small for him, and so he put on Joe's. Next, he pulled on gloves to protect his hands.

The shop was warm, the heat from the fire a bit overwhelming as he set metal into flame until it glowed an orange red. Next, he hammered it into the shape of a horseshoe on the steel anvil. The sound of his cross-peen hammer against the glowing metal filled the room, rewarding him with a sense of familiar satisfaction. He hammered, checked the metal, fired it up again and hammered some more, then he suddenly became aware of someone's presence. He didn't have to look toward the doorway to know who had entered the shop. "Annie," he said without looking up. "Do you need something?"

"Nay," she called back, to be heard over the ring of

iron against steel as he continued his work. "I've brought you a drink."

Jacob stopped pounding, set down his tools and glanced her way. "Water," he said with a grateful smile.

She carried the refreshments to the worktable on the opposite side of the room. "*Dat* said you'd be thirsty."

"*Ja,*" he said, watching her closely. "I could use a drink." She poured him a glass of water and offered it to him. He nodded his thanks and took a sip. "Just what I needed."

"I brought cookies, too." She placed the plate on the workbench within his reach. "For whenever you're hungry," she added. "*Dat* said you're to join us for lunch."

"You don't have to feed me," he said carefully.

"We've got plenty. So, you'll come? *Dat* will be pleased if you do."

"And you?" he dared to ask. "Will *you* mind?"

She blushed. "I'm asking you, aren't I?" Her expression became unreadable. "We're grateful that you're handling *Dat's* work."

"First see how I do before you're too grateful."

"*Dat* has confidence in your abilities, so I do, too." She touched a hand to her prayer *kapp*. "You will come?"

He noted the vibrant gold in her blond hair. "*Ja,* I'll be there. I wouldn't want to disappoint Joe." He locked gazes with her.

She looked away. "I'd better finish my chores—"

He glanced down at the cooling metal. He would have to fire it up again before he could continue the job. "And I better get back to work."

She hesitated. "If there is anything you need before then, come to the *haus* and let us know."

He nodded and turned his attention back to the forge, conscious of the exact moment when Annie left the shop.

Annie was stirring the pan of chicken potpie when she heard her brother's voice coming from the front of the house.

"Jacob!" Peter cried. "Come eat!"

Although she listened carefully, Annie couldn't hear his reply, but she recognized Jacob's deep male voice.

"Bread done?" *Mam* entered the room from the other side.

"Ja," Annie said. "Fresh from the oven and ready to be sliced. I took the butter out of the refrigerator."

"I'll open a jar of chow-chow," her mother said, referring to garden vegetables canned in a sweet-and-sour mix.

"I made a pitcher of iced tea this morning," Annie told her. "And lemonade." She filled a pitcher for those who preferred water.

Peter entered, followed closely by her father in his wheelchair. *"Dat*, I would have brought you something to eat." Her voice trailed off when she saw who stood behind the chair.

"Hallo," Jacob said as he pushed Joe's chair farther into the room. "It smells wonderful in here."

Mam turned from the kitchen counter with the dish of chow-chow. "I'm glad you could join us, Jacob."

"I'm happy you asked." He flashed Annie a look that made the heat rise in her face.

Annie scrambled to move furniture to accommodate her father's wheelchair at the table. Then she turned to the stove, where she ladled their meal into a large ceramic bowl. "I hope you like chicken potpie."

"Ja, 'tis one of my favorites." Jacob smiled as he took

the seat where instructed, next to her father. "Did *ya* make it?"

Annie shook her head. "*Nay, Mam* did."

"You helped with the pie squares," her *mam* said.

Annie had, in fact, rolled out the dough thinly, and she'd cut it into one-inch squares. Unlike the pie-crusted potpies made by the English, the Amish recipe for chicken potpie did not have a two-part flaky crust surrounding the cooked chicken and vegetables, nor was it baked in the oven. The women in their Amish community cooked the chicken in a stockpot until the meat was tender and the water became broth. Then they added vegetables and seasoning. Once the time was right, they stirred in pie squares, similar to the dough the English used in their chicken-and-dumpling recipes. Annie had learned the recipe from her mother at a young age, and over the years, she'd become skilled at making the thick, tasty dish.

The wonderful scent of chicken and the lingering aroma of baked bread permeated the kitchen, smelling delicious. Annie set the bowl on the table and went back for the bread. She placed the basket next to the main course.

The meal was simple, but there was plenty to eat. Annie put a hefty amount on each plate while her mother passed around the chow-chow bowl.

"Bread?" Annie extended the basket toward Jacob. "There's butter and strawberry jam."

Jacob smiled as he took a thick, crusty slice but he declined the toppings, apparently preferring to eat his bread plain.

"Where's Josiah?" her mother asked with a frown.

"He's coming. He's out in the fields," Annie told her.

She heard the front door open and footsteps as someone entered the house.

Joe smiled. "There he is now."

Annie saw her brother walk into the kitchen and note Jacob's presence.

"How goes it in the shop?" Josiah asked pleasantly as he took a seat next to Annie, who sat across from Jacob.

"Just getting used to it again," Jacob said, "but it's beginning to feel like home."

Her brother looked relieved, and her father appeared pleased. "Let me know if you need anything," Josiah said. He addressed his father. "It's nearly harvest time, *Dat.*"

Dat nodded. "Find out when the others are bringing in their crops. See if anyone can help out here one day."

Jacob spoke up, "Next week." He tore his bread in half. "We're all planning to come here on Tuesday."

"We'll need to cook and bake for the workers," her mother addressed Annie.

Annie nodded. "All the men are planning to help each other with the harvest?" she asked Jacob.

"Ja." Jacob forked up some noodles. "Everyone decided it would be quicker that way."

Annie silently agreed. Without help, it might take an Amish farmer and his sons several days to bring in their crops and properly store them. She had a feeling the community men had decided to pitch in at each farm because of her father, so that *Dat* would feel better about accepting help. "We should cook for the week."

Her mother picked up the breadbasket and passed it to her eldest son. Josiah took a piece and handed it to Peter. "I'll make dried-corn casserole," *Mam* said, "and macaroni salad to start."

The topic of conversation became centered on the harvest and how each family would have help each day, depending on the size of their land and their crops, and the offerings that the women of the house would bring to share at the community food table.

Annie decided to talk with Josie Mast, their neighbor, who together with her husband, William, knew most of what was happening within the Happiness community. Josie and William were always ready to lend a hand.

Annie remained conscious of Jacob at their kitchen table, enjoying his food and the conversation with her family. Across from him, she was able to study him unobtrusively. He looked solid and strong in his burgundy broadcloth shirt and *triblend* denim pants. He had removed his leather apron, as was appropriate, before coming to the house. He must have washed up outside, for there was no sign of soot or dirt on his face or hands. He'd undoubtedly left his hat in the shop, for his dark hair looked clean and shiny in the sun filtering in through the kitchen window.

He raised an eyebrow. Embarrassed to be caught examining him, she blushed and looked away. "Did everyone have enough to eat?" she asked as she rose. "There is plenty more on the stove."

When everyone claimed that they'd eaten enough of their meal, Annie left to retrieve dessert from the back room.

"Fresh apple pie," she said as she reentered the room, "with homemade ice cream."

While her family exclaimed their delight, it was Jacob's slow, appreciative smile that set her heart to racing. "I've been eager to taste your apple pie," he said.

After preparing several servings, Annie watched Jacob enjoy his portion and experienced a rush of satisfaction. All too soon, he was done eating, and he rose.

"Back to work," he said. "The meal was wonderful, topped off by a delicious dessert."

He didn't meet Annie's eyes as he thanked her parents for having him at their table. Then he left, and Annie noticed that the house seemed different with him gone. She didn't want to think about it too closely as she worked to put away food and clean up. As she was washing dishes, she thought about Jacob Lapp again and smiled.

"Annie," her mother said, "Preacher Levi will be coming for supper tomorrow night. What shall we make?"

Annie thought about it. The preacher was a frequent dinner guest. "Fried chicken?"

Mam nodded approvingly. "And make something special for dessert."

"Ja, Mam." Maybe a cobbler, she thought. She could use a jar of the peaches she'd canned this summer. She mentioned it to her mother.

"*Gut* idea, Annie. And let's make some sweet-and-vinegar green beans to go along with the chicken."

Her thoughts returned to Jacob. The meal with him had been pleasant. In the midst of her family, she'd been able to relax and truly appreciate his company. He'd been polite, teasing at times, occasionally catching her glance with a look that made her feel warm inside. She recalled Jacob the boy and couldn't help comparing him to the attractive man he'd become. She felt an infusion of heat. He was like a brother to her, she reminded herself.

Or was he?

Chapter Five

The sun shone warm and bright in a clear azure sky, and there was barely a breeze on harvest day at her family's farm. Annie stood outside next to her brother Josiah, watching as gray buggies drove down the lane toward the house and parked in a row in the barnyard. Other families came in horse-drawn wagons, some of which pulled farm equipment behind them. It was Monday instead of Tuesday, the day Annie and her family had expected the help. On Sunday, the community had decided to harvest their farm first after learning about her *dat's* appointment with the doctor on Tuesday. When they were done with their farm, the workers would move from one neighbor's farm property to the next, until everyone's crops were harvested.

Annie, her sister Barbara and her mother had spent hours cooking and baking to prepare for this week. Today the food would be served on tables set in the yard between their house and the *dawdi haus*—their *grosseldre's* cottage. Josiah and Peter with William Mast and Abram Peachy had set up tables of plywood on wooden sawhorses. Eli Shrock, Amos and Mae King's son-in-law, had brought the church's bench wagon earlier. Amos had come with Eli, and the two men, with Peter's help, had unloaded benches for everyone to sit on while they ate.

Annie set the tables with the linens that *Mam* used for such occasions. As the men and their families got out of their vehicles and approached, she felt satisfied that the day would go well. Josiah left her side to speak with Noah Lapp and his brother Eli, who had ridden in with his older brother and sister-in-law.

"Annie!" Rachel Lapp approached with a smile. She carried a large platter covered with plastic wrap.

"Cupcakes," Annie said with a grin. "The workers are going to love these."

Rachel glanced toward the food table, where Annie and her *mam* had put out breakfast for the crew. "You've been busy."

Annie gestured toward Rachel's cake dish. "So have you."

"Annie!" *Dat* sat on the porch in his wheelchair.

"Coming, *Dat*," she called back. She gave Rachel a half smile. "This is hard for him."

Rachel nodded. "Maybe if you push him closer so that he can watch the workers?"

"That's a great idea." Annie glanced toward her father. "I'll talk with you later." Rachel's husband, Noah, came up behind his wife. "Noah," she greeted him with a nod before she excused herself to help her father.

"*Dat?* You all right?" she asked as she climbed the porch steps.

"*Ja.*" Her father watched as families exited their vehicles, and the workers moved toward the field. "I should be out there helping."

She crouched before him, looked up. "*Dat*, you can't work, and everyone understands that. You need to stay here, and rest."

"Annie. Joe."

Annie turned and was startled to find Jacob Lapp on the stairs behind her. She rose quickly to her feet. "Jacob." She felt suddenly breathless. He looked ready for a full day's work in his royal blue shirt, navy coat and black suspenders and navy *triblend* denim pants. Her study of him fell to his black work boots before lifting up to his golden eyes.

"I thought Joe might like to watch us," Jacob said.

"I'd like that, Jake." Her father looked pleased. "Can't see anything from here."

Annie felt concerned, despite the fact that she thought the move a good idea. "What if you get tired?"

Her father smiled. "Then I'll have one of the boys bring me back."

"Not to worry, Annie," Jacob assured her. "I'll see that he rests if he needs it."

Annie didn't answer as she watched while Jacob pushed her father's chair down the ramp. She sighed. Until today, she hadn't seen or spoken with Jacob since he'd eaten lunch with them on his first day of work in her *dat's* blacksmith shop. According to her father, Jacob came to the shop each day, completed his work, then spoke briefly with her father before heading home. He'd been coming for days, but he hadn't bothered to stop into the house and say hello.

Why should he seek her out? He was helping her father, not her. It wasn't Jacob's fault that she couldn't stop thinking about him. Was it?

Annie sighed. There had to be an older man in the community who would make her a fine husband. Maybe if she prayed to the Lord He would show her her future husband. *Please, Lord, help and guide me. Help me to know Thy will.*

Mam came out of the house behind her. "Where's your *vadder*?"

Annie gestured toward the yard. "Jacob's taking *Dat* down for a better view." Once the workers continued to the other side of the farm, her father would no longer be able to watch them. *Maybe by then, Dat will be ready for a nap.*

Unbidden came a mental image of Jacob Lapp's smile. Annie pushed him from her mind as she went back into the house, where the women were preparing to set out more food.

"Will you be all right here?" Jacob asked Joe as he rolled the older man into a shady spot in the yard, with a good view.

"This is fine, Jacob." Joe stared as the workers walked into the field with their farm tools.

"Horseshoe Joe!" William Mast called. "How *ya* feeling?"

"Not too bad," Joe replied. "Doing as well as can be expected."

"You take care of yourself, and don't *ya* be worrying about anything. Your boy Josiah knows what he's doing, planning which areas to be covered by whom."

"I'm going to get to work, Joe," Jacob said. "I'll check back later to see how you are."

"I'd appreciate that." Joe seemed settled as he waved and answered his neighbors' and friends' inquiries about his recovery.

Jacob felt satisfied that Joe would be fine as he left to join his brothers Isaac and Eli. Minutes later, he grabbed his corn hook and climbed onto a wagon drawn by a team of Belgian horses. They headed toward the field area they'd been assigned. Isaac drove the team while

Jacob and Eli hand-husked corn. With each swipe of the hook, Jacob snagged a stalk, then cut off an ear, husked it quickly by hand and then he threw the cob into the back of the wagon. Jacob worked quickly, moving down the row, with Eli working beside him, to cut the crop from the stalks that Jacob missed. At the end of the row Isaac turned the wagon, and Jacob and Eli shifted to work the next row, cutting, husking and tossing the husked corn behind them.

In another area, workers shocked corn by using a horse-drawn binder that cut down the stalks to the ground. Men followed behind, gathering and then standing them on end, with their tops leaning together in tepee-like fashion. Still other community men worked with a corn picker that was pulled by horses. Cornstalks were pulled into the chain-driven machine, which mechanically removed the ears from the shoots and husks. The ears were tossed through a passageway into a wagon pulled behind the picker. Only a few knew how to work the equipment, which could jam and be dangerous, especially its chains, which gathered the crop.

Jacob preferred husking the corn by hand. It might seem time-consuming, but each ear that was tossed into the back was ready to be dried before it was stored. He had shocked corn, as well, and he felt satisfaction in seeing the tents of stalks, in rows along the fields.

"We should get this acreage done before the midday meal," Eli commented as he bent to the work.

"*Ja*, but there is still the hay to bring in." Jacob inspected the corn he'd just shocked and, satisfied, threw it in with the others before he reached for another. "Although we'll have plenty of help."

"*Ja*. It won't take long, not with everyone pitching in."

Eli hand-husked from another stalk and tossed the clean ears in the back of the wagon.

They worked for a time, then decided to break for lunch. Jacob accompanied his twin brother back to the house and the food waiting there. Isaac stayed with the team and waited for them to return with food for him.

"How are things with Annie?" Eli asked.

"I barely see her," Jacob replied, taking off his hat and wiping his brow with his shirtsleeve.

"Is staying away your doing or hers?"

Jacob shrugged. "I've been busy. Why would I seek her out?"

"Because you like her," Eli said with quiet understanding.

"I'm keeping my distance and getting the job done. That's all I need to do until I'm finished at the smithy."

"That could be a long time, Jake." Eli gestured toward Annie, who was arranging baked goods on the dessert table.

"I'll manage," he said. Somehow he would work hard, keep his distance from Joe's daughter and, in so doing, protect his heart. Not a chance that he'd be disappointed again by Anna Marie Zook.

"If you say so, Jake," his brother said, but he sounded unconvinced.

Annie stood by the dessert table, ready to slice a piece of cake or pie for a worker when she saw Jedidiah Lapp chatting with his wife, Sarah. She watched them a moment—she couldn't help herself. She'd been heartbroken when Jed had broken up with her years before, and she'd hurt from the loss when last year he'd courted and married Sarah Mast, William Mast's cousin from Delaware.

Watching the affection between them, the way he placed a hand on her arm, the soft smiles they exchanged, Annie felt pain. Seeing the two of them together was a reminder of what she didn't have. She wasn't jealous. She understood now that Sarah and Jed's marriage was God ordained.

Annie wanted a husband—and a family. As *Mam* had pointed out, she wasn't getting any younger. But how could she marry when no one showed an interest in her? She blinked back tears. She'd work hard to be a wife whom a husband would appreciate. She wanted children, to hold a baby in her arms, a child to nurture and love.

She sniffed, looked down and straightened the plates. The drinks were on one end—pitchers and jugs of iced tea and lemonade, and there were bottles of birch beer and cola.

"May I have some lemonade?" a deep, familiar voice said.

Annie felt a jolt and looked up. "Jacob." His expression was serious as he eyed her. She glanced down and noticed the fine dusting of corn residue on his dark jacket. "Lemonade?" she echoed self-consciously.

"*Ja.* Lemonade," he said with amusement.

She nodded and quickly reached for the pitcher. She kept her eyes on the task as she poured his drink into a plastic cup, only chancing a glance at him when she handed it to him.

"How is the work going?" she asked conversationally.

"We are nearly finished with the corn. We'll be cutting hay next." He lifted the cup to his lips and took a swallow.

Warmth pooled in her stomach as she watched the movement of his throat. "How's *Dat*?" she asked. She had seen him chatting with her father earlier.

With a small smile, Jacob glanced toward her *dat*. "He

says he's not tired. He claims he's enjoying the view too much." His smile dissipated. "He'll be exhausted later."

Annie agreed. "I'll check on him in a while." She hesitated. "Are you hungry? I can fix you a plate—"

His striking golden eyes met hers for several heartbeats. "*Nay*, I'll fix one myself." He finished his drink and held out his cup to her. "May I?"

Heart pumping hard, she hurried to refill it. With a crooked smile and a nod of thanks, Jacob accepted the refreshment and left. The warm flutter in her stomach became a painful burning as she watched him walk away, stopping briefly to chat with Noah and Rachel, his brother and sister-in-law, at another table.

She thought about their conversation. He seemed different, but then she hadn't seen much of him since that first day. She had stayed away from the shop. She didn't want to interrupt him when he was hard at work. Her sister Barbara had been the one to offer him meals lately, and Barbara had informed them that he'd accepted a snack, but that he'd been bringing a packed lunch from home.

Annie followed his progress as he headed toward the food table, grabbed a plate and talked with Josie Mast, who stood behind the table and served up his supper.

"Annie." Rachel smiled at her as she approached. "You look thoughtful."

Annie nodded. "Rachel, have you ever felt like you've done something wrong and don't know how to make it right?"

"*Ja*, years ago when I was hospitalized after Abraham Beiler's courting buggy slipped off an icy road, and I was thrown into a ditch."

Annie had heard about the accident not long after Rachel, the new schoolteacher, had arrived in Happiness. "Why did you feel as if you'd done something wrong?"

"After the accident, Abraham never came to visit me in the hospital—not once, even though we were sweethearts. I wondered what I had done to ruin his affection for me. And I mistakenly felt as if I was being punished."

Annie felt sympathy for what Rachel had suffered. "That must have been awful."

Rachel nodded. "But then God brought me Noah. Things happen to us that we can't control," she continued. "I believe that the Lord has a plan for us. He watches over us and gives us strength when we most need it. I know now that Abraham and I were not meant to be together. It is Noah who God chose for me, and I am grateful to the Lord for giving him to me."

"*Ja*, you and Noah are meant to be," Annie said with a smile. "As Sarah and Jed are."

Rachel grinned. "As there is someone God has chosen for you. You just don't know who yet."

Annie glanced toward the food table, where several men were having plates of meat, vegetables and sides dished up for them. "I pray the Lord finds me someone soon," she confessed softly. She felt Rachel's sympathetic touch on her arm.

"I believe it will happen." Rachel looked back to see the line of workers. "I'd better help out Josie."

"You're a kind person, Rachel." Annie smiled at the young woman with genuine warmth.

"So are you, Annie. You're a *gut* daughter and sister, and you're always willing to help anyone."

As she watched Rachel join Josie on the other side of the room, Annie thought of her behavior toward Jacob. She caught sight of him with his brother Eli. The contrast of Jacob's dark hair and Eli's light locks struck her, making her think of their differences and similarities as they disappeared into the barn. They came out a few minutes later, Eli carrying tools, Jacob leading Nosey, one of her father's workhorses.

As if he sensed her regard, Jacob glanced in her direction. She started to lift a hand to wave, but the somber look in his expression stopped her.

The workers completed the fall harvest at their farm. Annie watched as her fellow church members packed up their belongings and left with their families. William Mast waved as he drove his shock wagon with its team of mules away from the fields, past the house.

His wife, Josie, exited behind her. "We finished wrapping the leftovers."

"I'll help carry them out to your buggy," Annie offered.

"*Nay*, you'll be keeping them."

"But everyone will be at your farm next." She straightened her head covering.

Josie smiled. "*Ja*, and everyone has been cooking and baking to prepare for tomorrow, as well."

Annie nodded. It was true. She, *Mam* and Barbara had made several cakes and pies for the week's harvesting, as well as potato salad, dried-corn casserole and sweet-and-vinegar green beans.

"We appreciate the help," Annie said softly. She fondly regarded her father, who still sat in his wheelchair in the yard. All day he had refused to come inside to rest.

"How is he feeling?" Josie asked, her voice quiet.

Annie frowned. "He believes he is mending too slowly. He thinks he should be walking again."

"He is rushing his recovery. It bothers him to see others do his work."

"*Ja.* I wish I could help him. *Mam* has loving patience, but it has been difficult. *Dat* is a *gut* man, but this has been hard for him."

Josie's touch on her arm comforted her. "Things will get better."

Annie agreed. With God's help, everything was possible.

"We'll be heading home. *Ellen!*" Josie called into the house for her daughter.

Within seconds, Josie and William's twelve-year-old daughter, Ellen, exited the residence. "*Mam*, Miriam insisted we take this cake for *Dat.*"

Annie smiled. "It's William's favorite."

Josie hesitated and then grinned. "If Miriam insists." She called for her two sons, who had been playing ball with Abram Peachy's boys. "Will! Elam! Time to go!"

Annie watched with a smile as the Mast boys climbed into their family buggy, followed by their mother and sister. She waved as they left and followed the buggy's progress as it headed along the long dirt drive toward the main road.

Soon, other families followed suit, gathering their children before going home. It had been a wonderful day, Annie realized. She enjoyed her church community, the way everyone was there to help when someone needed it.

Annie entered the kitchen to find her mother and Katie Lapp seated at the table, sharing a pot of tea. Millie lay curled up in the corner.

"Annie," Katie said with a smile, "will you join us?"

"*Ja.*" Annie pulled out a chair. "Where is Barbara?" Her sister had been out of sight for most of the day.

Mam poured her a cup of tea. "She's upstairs gathering the boys' clothes for washing."

Annie rose to her feet. "I'll help her."

Her mother placed a hand on her arm. "*Nay*, Annie. Sit. There is no hurry to do the wash. This is Barbara's doing."

Annie felt concern. "*Mam*, what's bothering her? She's been quiet and doesn't talk with me like she used to." Barbara had seemed distant ever since her return last week from their great-aunt's house in New Wilmington. Her sister and she had always been close, but something had changed. Annie knew she'd been spending a lot of time with her father. Did Barbara feel slighted?

"Your sister spent time with a boy in New Wilmington," *Mam* said.

Annie widened her eyes. "She didn't tell me. She used to tell me everything." She reached for the sugar bowl, moved it closer to her cup.

"She got her feelings hurt. David chose another girl to be his sweetheart, someone from his local church community."

"I didn't know. Why didn't she tell me?" Annie repeated as she stirred a spoonful of sugar into her tea.

"Embarrassed maybe," Katie suggested. "You're her older sister. She may have thought you'd think her foolish."

"She didn't know the boy long," *Mam* said.

"But long enough to lose her heart and have it broken," Annie said with a new realization of why Barbara had been acting strangely. She would have to talk with her sister in private. Tell her that she understood how Barbara felt.

Barbara entered the room as she rearranged the garments she carried over one arm. "*Mam*, I found Peter's clothes on the bedroom floor. He's in the shower—" She looked up and stopped when she saw *Mam*, Katie Lapp and Annie seated at the table.

"Want a cup of tea?" Annie invited with a smile.

"The clothes—" Her sister appeared anxious.

"Put them in the washer, Barbara," *Mam* said. "We can take care of them later."

Barbara crossed toward the back room, where the propane freezer and washing machine were kept. Annie heard the clink of the lid lifted, and the thump seconds later after her sister had dropped it closed.

Annie smiled encouragingly at her sister as Barbara reentered the kitchen. She pulled out a chair for her and then rose to take another teacup from the cabinet. "Anyone want a cookie?" she asked.

"Not me," *Mam* said.

"I'll have one," Katie replied, and Barbara agreed that she'd have one, too.

"Where's *Dat*?" Barbara asked as she accepted the tea that Annie poured for her.

"He's still out in the yard." Annie stood. "I should check on him."

"No need," a deep voice said, making Annie jerk.

She turned to see Jacob Lapp behind her father's wheelchair. Heart thumping hard, she focused on her father. *"Dat."* Unable to help herself, she felt drawn to the younger man. "Jacob. I didn't hear you come in."

"Joe." Her mother rose and hurried to his side. "You must be tired."

"I'm fine, Miriam." Her father smiled and Annie was pleased to see him happy. "Jacob has asked me to help out in the shop next week."

Annie frowned. "Are you sure that's a *gut* idea?"

"I told him only for an hour." Jacob held her glance briefly before he looked away. Annie felt a sniggle of disappointment.

Mam examined *Dat's* face and nodded. "That would be *gut*." Annie saw her smile gratefully at Jacob.

Josiah entered the kitchen. "I've brought in the mail." He flipped through the envelopes and then frowned as he drew out one in particular. He handed it to *Dat*. "From the hospital."

Annie watched her father as he opened the envelope. He turned pale as he read the bill. She saw how he fought to compose himself as he refolded the paper and stuffed it back in.

"Joe," Katie said as she stood with her teacup in hand, "whatever it is, you know our church community will pay the expense."

"This is too much, even for our community," *Dat* said wearily.

"Then we'll hold fund-raisers. As many as it will take to pay your bill." Katie took her cup to the sink and washed it.

Samuel, Jacob's father and Jacob's twin brother, Eli, entered the kitchen. "What's wrong?" his *dat* asked as if sensing the tension in the room.

"Joe received his hospital bill in today's mail," Katie said as she returned to her seat, and Annie saw her flash a concerned glance toward *Mam*.

Samuel placed a hand on his friend's shoulder. "Don't *ya* worry, Joe. We'll find a way. The burden isn't yours alone."

Joe nodded but remained silent. Annie saw the look on her father's face; any happiness he'd had at joining Jacob in the shop next week had disappeared under the weight of debt.

"Don't worry, Joe. We're all here for you," Jacob said, and Annie looked at him with gratitude. When he favored her with a warm smile, she felt her stomach flip-flop.

Annie looked away, her heart racing as the Lapps got ready to leave a few minutes later. They would gather at the Masts the next day and then move on to Abram Peachy's place after bringing in the harvest there.

It would be a busy week, but she would be seeing Jacob every day. She felt a wash of pleasure that turned to fear as she recognized a subtle shift in her feelings toward him.

Jacob stood by the buggy, grabbed hold to lift himself in. But then he paused to glance in her direction, and she experienced the startling impact of his golden regard. Heart hammering hard, she raised a hand to wave. She inhaled sharply when he grinned, touched the edge of his hat brim as he acknowledged her with a dip of his head.

"Tomorrow," he mouthed.

Her spine tingled as she moved her lips, "Tomorrow."

Chapter Six

Annie's *Dat* was sleeping late; yesterday's church service and this past week's busy harvest had tired him. *Mam* thought he would easily stay abed until nine o'clock, a late hour for someone who usually got up at five in the morning before his accident. *Mam* and Barbara were busy at *Grossmudder's* house, leaving Annie at home in the kitchen, baking fresh cinnamon rolls. Peter had gone to the Masts to help William paint the rear side of his barn. Josiah, having finished his morning chores, had gone to visit his sweetheart Nancy King.

Annie felt a sense of purpose. She hurriedly filled a thermos with coffee and placed two warm cinnamon rolls on a plate. With peace offerings in hand, she headed out to the shop to talk with Jacob, a funny feeling in the pit of her stomach as she approached. She heard the ring of steel against steel as she neared the shop door. Annie paused at the threshold to observe Jacob work.

With royal blue shirtsleeves rolled up to reveal his forearms and a leather blacksmith's apron tied about his neck and his waist, Jacob held the piece of metal within the tongs, examining it from every direction. Annie didn't think he noticed her as he fired up a propane blowtorch, held it against the piece of iron, before turning off the torch and then transferring the glowing metal back onto the anvil. He raised his hammer and banged the iron into shape. Suddenly, as if he sensed her presence, he looked up and without a smile set down the metal, tongs and hammer. He stepped away from the anvil and gave a polite nod.

"Annie." He had taken off his hat and hung it on a wall peg, and his dark hair looked a bit mussed as if he'd run his fingers through it.

She offered him a tentative smile, raised the thermos and plate. "I brought you coffee and cinnamon rolls." She held her breath, expecting him to refuse her offering.

A gleam entered his golden eyes. "Homemade?"

She gave him a genuine smile. "Is there any other kind?" She approached and handed him the plate. "May I pour your coffee?"

Watching her carefully, he inclined his head. "I didn't expect this."

"I know I haven't been in to talk with you," she began as she unscrewed the cap and filled his cup. She kept her eyes on the steam wafting from the hot brew as she extended it toward him.

"You came to talk?" he asked as he accepted the drink. "About what?" He appeared interested as he sipped the coffee.

Annie looked away in a sudden rush of uncertainty. Then she forced herself to look straight into his eyes. "I owe you an apology," she began confidently. "You were nothing but kind to me after *Dat* had his accident, and I was rude and ungrateful—" She felt the heat rise in her cheeks but met his glance head-on. "I'm sorry. I am very grateful for what you did for *Dat*. We all are. The Lord can't be happy with me."

He didn't laugh, didn't smile. He considered her as if he were searching the depths of her soul, and she shifted uneasily. "No apology needed," he finally said. He drank from his cup again.

"*Ja*, there is," she said. She wanted them to be friends like they were when they were children.

Jacob picked up a frosted cinnamon roll and viewed it from every angle. "This would be a *gut* apology if I needed one," he said before he took a bite. She watched him chew and swallow with great enjoyment. "Fortunately, I don't need one."

Annie watched him with confusion. She was surprised that he had brushed off her rudeness. She felt the tension within her ease, wondered why she was relieved and why making friends with Jacob should matter to her so much.

He took another drink. "How did you know how I like my coffee?"

She felt the focus of his golden eyes on her. "I saw you make it for yourself one day."

He looked surprised but pleased. "Do you want a cinnamon roll?"

She shook her head. "*Nay*, I brought them for you."

"I'm happy to share," he said with a smile, and Annie felt her heart beat rapidly. He extended the bun but she shook her head. "Will your *vadder* be coming in today?"

"*Ja*," she said. "He slept late this morning. He will be over later. It was nice of you to ask him to come. But it won't be easy having him here when you're trying to get work done."

"Has he been underfoot in the house?" Jacob jumped up to sit on the top of the worktable.

His easy movements drew Annie's attention to his muscled arms and long legs. "*Nay. Dat* has no wish to interfere with our housework. But the shop—that is his place. He is bound to give advice—some of it unwanted."

"That's where you're wrong, Annie. I learned a lot from your *vadder*. I spent hours taking his advice. It will be a pleasure to have him here."

"And he will love being here again. His heart has always been with forging metal, more so than with farmwork."

Jacob nodded. "He has your brothers to handle the farm for him. It is a *gut* arrangement."

Silence reigned for several seconds, and Annie began to feel self-conscious.

"You know Jed and Sarah are happy together," he said suddenly, the non sequitur startling her.

"Ja." She blinked, felt her face burn. "Their marriage is God ordained."

"You believe that?" He eyed her skeptically over his cinnamon roll.

"Ja, I do." She examined him without embarrassment. "Why do you doubt it?"

"You were Jed's sweetheart."

"For a short time," she said, feeling a little pang at the memory, "but it wasn't meant to be."

Jacob sipped from his coffee and set the cup down on the table beside him. "Last Monday, during the harvest, I saw you watching him. It brought you tears."

Annie reached up to finger the string on her prayer *kapp.* "I know I shouldn't, but I was wishing I had someone, too, that I could be as happy as Jed and Sarah, and Noah and Rachel." She bit her lip. "I hope to marry…" she trailed off. She had no business telling him about her plan to marry an older church member, to have a happy marriage like Charlotte had with Abram Peachy.

"You hope to marry whom?" he prompted softly.

Embarrassed, she looked down at her shoes. "I've decided it would be best for me to marry someone older within our church district. Someone like Abram Peachy."

"Abram is married to Charlotte."

She gave him a look. "I know. I merely want to have a family like Charlotte does." *To have someone accept me for who I am, to look at me with quiet love and contentment.*

"And you believe that you will find happiness by wedding an older man?" His voice was soft.

Annie nodded. She would care for her husband, enjoy a safe kind of peaceful affection. She would know that with him, she'd never have to worry about a broken heart. And as time went on, her fondness for him would grow into a deep, abiding love. She was silent as her mind raced with images of her future.

"Annie." Jacob's deep voice drew her from her thoughts. "Is something wrong?"

She shook her head, feeling foolish. "*Nay.* I am fine." She felt suddenly uncomfortable for all she'd revealed to him. "I should go back to the *haus.* I have work to do." She gave him a slight smile. "*Dat* will be out after breakfast." She turned to leave.

"Annie—"

She stopped and spun around.

"Your *dat*, he is all right?"

She was pleased by his concern. Her discomfort eased. "He is worried about his medical expenses."

"We will raise the money." Jacob set down the plate and pushed off the worktable.

"I know, but it worries him still. He feels that he made a grave error in trying to fix the roof."

"We all make mistakes. He was doing a *gut* thing— that is never a mistake."

"*Danki*, Jacob," she said. He raised an eyebrow in question. "For helping *Dat*," she added. She turned to leave.

"Annie," he called. She paused and faced him. "I sincerely doubt the Lord is angry or upset with you."

She blushed. She didn't know what to say. So she remained silent as she hurried to escape his intense regard and startling words.

The women of the community met on Wednesday to plan a fund-raiser dinner for Horseshoe Joe. Annie, her sister Barbara, and *Mam* sat in Katie Lapp's gathering room, listening to the others talk.

"We can do a breakfast or supper," Alta Hershberger said. Alta was Annie's aunt, whose late husband had been *Mam's* brother. The woman was kind but a bit of a busybody. She had two daughters, Mary and Sally, and it was Alta's deepest wish to see each of her girls settled with a husband and family.

"Supper would be best, I think." Mae King jotted down some notes on a small pad. "Fried chicken? What else?"

"The English love chicken and dumplings. We could make that." Josie Mast sat in the chair next to Annie's. She raised her cup of tea to her lips, took a sip.

"We should keep it simple, but we do need to consider who will come and what the English like to eat," Katie said as she entered the room with two plates of cookies. "Rachel made these," she murmured as she extended the plate to Annie and her mother.

Annie and Rachel exchanged looks across the room. Rachel winked and gifted her with a smile.

"Do you think dinner is the best way to go? We can

serve breakfast with muffins and pancakes, waffles, eggs and toast." It was Charlotte Peachy who spoke up.

"It would be easier, I suppose," *Mam* said.

"I think we should do a supper first, then later do a breakfast," Nancy King said as she rose to grab a small plate on which she put three of Rachel's homemade cookies.

There were fifteen women in the room. They had a brief discussion on the merits of hosting a supper versus a breakfast. Annie watched the women with a small smile. Nancy King caught her eye, and her lips curved up in shared amusement.

The women's conversation stopped abruptly when Samuel and his twin sons entered the room. The silence seemed deafening to Annie.

Samuel looked at his wife. "A meeting?"

Katie nodded. "To discuss the fund-raiser for Horseshoe Joe."

Samuel appeared pleased. "A supper?"

Annie was conscious of Jacob and Eli, standing behind their father. To her dismay, Annie found her interest taken up mostly with the dark-haired twin with the stunning golden eyes. "Supper or breakfast—we're trying to decide."

"Why not do a supper first?" Samuel suggested. "Hold it on a Friday evening? The English enjoy eating out on Friday nights."

Jacob stepped forward, and Annie got a good view of his handsome face. He towered over his father by five inches. Eli was as tall as Jacob, but there the similarity in their appearances ended. "Jacob. Eli," Annie dared to speak up. "What do you think we should do—a supper or a breakfast?" She felt a flush of warmth as Jacob studied her as he mulled it over. When he didn't answer immediately, she turned quickly to focus on his fraternal twin, but Eli was busy discussing the merits of whether or not to host a supper with her sister Barbara.

After much discussion, the community women decided to hold a chicken supper the following week on a Friday night. Samuel and his sons left, and Annie was able to relax and plan the dishes her family would contribute.

Soon, *Mam* and Barbara were ready to leave. Annie stood and finished a conversation with Rachel and her sister-in-law Sarah. "We'll bring the desserts," Sarah said and Rachel agreed. "Sarah loves to bake, and she's good at it."

Annie nodded. "So are you," she said. She smiled at Sarah. "I've had a piece of your chocolate cream pie," she admitted. She no longer felt awkward in Sarah's company. She had told Jacob the truth; she had come to accept Jed and Sarah's marriage. Seeing them together no longer upset her.

As she left the house, Annie saw Abram Peachy helping his wife into their family buggy. "They are happy together—Charlotte and Abram."

"Ja," Rachel said from beside her. "I've never seen Charlotte happier, and she loves the children. Little Ruthie took to her from the start. It's hard to believe how much Ruthie has grown. She's nearly six."

"There she is with her brother Nate," Annie observed.

They stood silently for a moment, then Noah came out of the barn with Jacob.

"Time for home." Rachel smiled at her husband as he approached.

Annie saw the way Noah looked at Rachel and the warmth in his wife's expression as she regarded him with affection. They were fortunate to have found each other.

She watched as families departed, enjoying the view, feeling a bit wistful that she had no husband or children to share her life. Suddenly, she realized that she was no longer alone. Jacob stood behind and within a few feet of her. She glanced over her shoulder, then turned to face him. "Jacob."

"Annie." His lips curved upward. "Why are you standing out here all alone?

Because I have no one to call my own, she thought. "I'm enjoying the view."

He shook his head as if he were disappointed. "Come into the *haus*. Your *mudder* and sister are still inside."

Silently, she followed him in. "*Mam*, are we staying for a while?" Annie asked, conscious of Jacob next to her.

"*Nay*, 'tis time to leave." *Mam* stood. "We have much to do for this fund-raiser. Katie, *danki* for everything."

Jacob's mother nodded. "'Tis my pleasure, Miriam. I will talk with you later to finalize the fund-raiser menu."

Her mother glanced in Jacob's direction as she, Annie and Jacob exited the house. "Jacob. It's *gut* to see you again as always. How are things going in the shop?"

"*Gut*. Horseshoe Joe is an excellent teacher. I feel as if I'd never left."

"Has he been behaving?" *Mam* paused on the front porch.

"*Ja*. It's *gut* to have his company," Jacob said. "I feel like a young boy again, learning how to tackle various jobs."

"What kind of jobs?" Annie wanted to know. She was curious and in no hurry to leave.

"There is a certain skill in reworking an old horseshoe to extend its use," he said as he peered out into the yard, before refocusing his attention on Annie. "He's been teaching me how to create more traction on the bottom of an older worn horseshoe." He smiled. "For your *vadder*, it's an easy thing. I've become accustomed to the work now, though."

Jacob seemed to enjoy his surroundings. It was clear that he loved his family. Earlier, his eyes had been soft as he'd looked about the gathering room, apparently studying all the ladies who had come to meet in his parents' house. For a long minute, Annie hadn't been able to take her eyes off him. As was the custom, he had hung up his hat when he'd come inside. He had retrieved his hat and held it by the brim. His dark hair was shiny and looked newly combed. He wore a maroon shirt and navy *triblend* denim pants, held up by dark suspenders. His shirtsleeves were rolled up slightly, revealing strong, muscled forearms.

"We'd better get home," *Mam* said as she continued down the steps. "Peter is waiting for us. He has chores to do, and I know he's eager to get started. He won't leave your *vadder* alone."

"Take care, Jacob," Annie said softly as she followed her mother.

"I'll be at the shop tomorrow," he said. "Maybe I will see you then."

Pleased by his parting words, Annie joined her mother and sister near the buggy. She climbed into the front seat and picked up the leathers. *Mam* sat up front on the other side, while Barbara took a seat in the back.

As if unable to help herself, Annie glanced toward the Lapps' front porch. There Jacob stood, watching her. With a funny feeling in her chest, she waved and felt glad when he lifted a hand in response. Although she somehow managed to carry on an easy conversation with her sister and mother during the buggy ride home, she couldn't get him out of her mind.

* * *

A week later, Jacob stood in the doorway of Abram Peachy's barn, wondering how they were going to set up the tables for the dinner fund-raiser. He heard the rumble of an engine and stepped outside as a large flatbed truck was backing up to the barn. His father directed the vehicle into position, until with a call of "ho!" he instructed the truck to halt.

Jacob was surprised by what the truck carried: long banquet tables and plastic chairs.

When the vehicle came to a complete halt, the passenger door opened and his brother Jed hopped out. He came to where they stood at the back of the truck. "Matt is on the volunteer fire department. The men wanted to help, so they offered us the use of these—no charge."

Samuel looked pleased. "That is kind of them."

The driver shut off the engine and climbed out of the vehicle. Matt was Jed's construction-job foreman.

"What do you think?" he asked with a grin.

"We can certainly use these. Thanks," Jacob said to the *Englisher*. He reached onto the truck and pulled off two chairs, which he leaned against the barn. Other available workers followed suit, hauling out the furniture and setting them with the rest.

As he worked to prepare the area inside the large fairly new space that was Abram's barn and church-gathering place, Jacob thought of the women who would be arriving soon to ready the tables. He imagined Annie carefully spreading linens over every available banquet surface and then arranging each place setting with care. That was something he'd noticed about her whenever he visited the Zook farmhouse. Whether it was serving cookies and iced tea or cake and coffee, she took care in whatever she did, making a plate of goodies look nice or re-membering what he liked in his coffee.

Annie. The way she was always in his thoughts, he was in dangerous territory. He mustn't make the same mistake twice. He had loved her once, only to get his heart trounced. He couldn't afford to fall for Annie a second time.

A buggy pulled into the barnyard and Annie stepped out. Jacob drew a sharp breath. *Dear Lord, keep me strong. Keep me safe from loving Annie.*

He watched her approach and felt a hard jolt. It was too late. He had fallen in love with Annie, and he didn't know how he was going to get over her a second time.

Chapter Seven

Annie climbed out of her family's buggy and then reached in for the box of tablecloths, plates, eating utensils and napkins. She turned toward the barn. "It looks like they're just setting up the tables now," she said to her sister.

"*Ja.* There is Josiah," Barbara said. "Look! They have long tables and folding chairs!"

Annie nodded, but her attention wasn't on the furniture being unloaded from the back of the truck. It was on the men doing the work—her brother Josiah, Amos King, Samuel Lapp and his sons—and Levi Stoltzfus who had come to help out. She looked from one man to the other, settling briefly on Jacob before quickly moving on. Levi glanced over and waved. Annie grinned and waved back. She was happy to see him. She always felt comfortable in his company.

"Girls, hold up," *Mam* said. "What are we going to do about these pies and cakes?"

Annie turned carefully, her arms full. "Why not leave them where they are until we can get one of the food tables set up? Unless you want to ask Charlotte if we can store them in her pantry."

Mam nodded. "If we leave them here, the boys are liable to find and eat them."

Annie agreed. Cradling the box of items, she approached the barn. "Noah," she greeted. "Amos. Samuel." Her heart skipped a beat as she and Jacob locked gazes. *"Hallo,* Jacob."

"That box looks heavy," Jacob said as he reached out to take it from her.

"Danki." She followed him inside the barn and checked the placement of furniture.

She saw Jacob study the room. "Where would ya like me to put this?"

Annie gestured toward a table along the wall. "There would be fine." He set the box down and she managed a smile for him when he faced her. "The room looks *gut.* We'll be able to handle a lot of paying guests. Who gave us the use of all this?"

"The fire department. Jed's construction foreman, Matt Rhoades, is a member."

"Gut, gut," she said. "The English will be more comfortable on chairs than on our benches."

"Ja," he agreed and she could sense him studying her as she inspected the room.

His scrutiny made her feel suddenly uncomfortable. "I should get to work. I have a lot of to prepare."

He nodded. "I have things to do, as well."

"I appreciate the help," she offered as he started to walk away.

He stopped, glanced back. "'Twas my pleasure, Annie," he said silkily.

Heart thumping hard, Annie watched him walk away. She had to focus on the task at hand. She drew in a steadying breath as she reached into the box for the tablecloths. Instead of plastic, the churchwomen had decided to use linens instead. She envisioned how the room would look when the tables were covered and place settings done and felt pleased.

"Annie, where are the plates and napkins?" Barbara asked. Annie hadn't missed her sister's approach. She gestured toward the box.

Barbara flashed a grin as she headed toward it. Their relationship was back to normal after a sisterly discussion last week. They shared a bedroom, and one evening, after they'd gone upstairs to bed, Annie had broached the subject of David Byler, the boy Barbara had fallen for during her visit to their great-aunt Evie's in northern Pennsylvania. At first, Barbara had been upset, almost defensive, until Annie had offered sympathy while talking of her own heartbreak over Jedidiah Lapp.

"I feel foolish, Annie," Barbara had whispered into the dark silence of their bedroom. They not only shared a room but a bed large enough for two.

"Why?" Annie had asked. "Because you fell in love? There is nothing wrong with loving someone." They had lain side by side in their white cotton nightgowns, their hair free from their head coverings, unpinned and flowing well down their backs—Annie's golden blond and Barbara's rich dark brown. When she was younger, Annie had shared a room with Joan, their eldest sister. Joan had lain next to her each night and shared private, whispered conversations, usually about the boy Joan liked and later married, while other times they had discussed Annie's feelings for Jedidiah Lapp. Barbara and she, closer in age than Joan and her, shared a friendship beyond being sisters. Barbara's distance from her after she'd returned from her trip with their *grosseldres* had hurt. Once she'd learned the truth of Barbara's painful experience, she was able to offer her sister kindness and understanding—and the assurance that Barbara had neither been foolish nor rash.

As she and Barbara worked together to set up the tables for tonight's dinner fundraiser, Annie felt good. She had missed their quiet conversations. Now they gave each other frequent smiles as they discussed how to arrange each place setting.

Annie stood back to admire their handiwork. "We need five more tablecloths."

"Katie Lapp mentioned bringing more, in case we need them," Barbara said.

"So did Mae King."

Several women entered the room, among them their mother, Miriam, with Katie and Mae. Each woman carried a metal rack with an aluminum chafing dish and a can of gelled cooking fuel.

"The room looks *gut*," *Mam* stated as she approached.

"We need more tablecloths," Barbara said.

"The extras are in the buggy," Katie said. "Noah told me about the tables and chairs."

Mae King set down the chafing dish. "I hope we have a *gut* turnout."

"I think we will," Katie said. "We've had over a week to get the word out. The boys put posters in all the local stores and in the shops at the Rockvale Outlet Mall and Tanger Outlets. Bob Whittier told everyone who came into his store."

"I hope so." Annie wanted this fund-raiser to be a success for her father's sake. *Dat's* worry over his medical bills was taking a toll on his recovery.

"After we're done setting up, we'll head home," *Mam* said. "Later, we'll come back with the food, an hour and a half before dinner starts."

Alta Hershberger entered the barn. "Miriam, the place looks nice."

Mam smiled. "It should do the job."

"Where do you want these?" Annie's aunt seemed genuinely happy to help out.

Mae gestured toward a table. The women discussed the arrangements. Except for the dessert portion of the meal afterward, they would be serving their guests. Several side items would be set out family style while the younger women, including Annie, Barbara, Nancy King and young Ellen Mast, would be on hand to make sure that no one left hungry.

The women finished dinner preparations and departed. Annie, Barbara and their mother discussed the fund-raiser as they drove home in their buggy.

"We have plenty of seats for our guests," Barbara said.

"*Ja*, now we should pray that we see a *gut* profit."

"'Tis a fair price, *Mam*," Annie said. She directed the mare onto their dirt driveway. "Rick Martin's bringing his family, and he told his friends. The dinner fund-raiser will be successful."

"I pray that it will be so," *Mam* said somberly.

Annie reached out to clasp *Mam's* hand. "I have faith, *Mam*. You must, too." She drove skillfully down the drive and into the barnyard. Josiah and Peter had returned home earlier in their market wagon. She lifted a hand to smile and wave at Josiah in the yard. "The Lord will guide us in our time of need," she told her mother. "He has been *gut* to us. *Dat's* injuries could have been worse."

The silence in the buggy, as the vehicle came to a complete stop, felt heavy. Annie thought of what might have happened if her father had injured himself more severely. What if he'd broken his neck or cracked his skull?

"We have a lot to be thankful for." *Mam* smiled at her as she climbed out. "Come, we have much to do yet."

The fund-raiser was a success. Jacob stood near the door and watched as the diners enjoyed the dinner prepared by the women of the Happiness Amish community. Earlier, he had gone home to wash and change his clothes. He looked for where he might be able to help. He observed the young women—including Annie—attending to their dinner guests.

There were bowls of sides on the tables: potato salad, green beans, coleslaw, dried-corn casserole, sweet-and-sour chow-chow and fresh home-baked bread. The women went from guest to guest to inquire about their choice of meat—fried chicken, roasted chicken or roast beef—and whether or not they preferred other sides.

So far the people who'd come were pleasant. The first to arrive had been the Zooks' neighbors, Rick Martin and his wife and children—a teenage son and daughter. Store-owner Bob Whittier, with his brood, came soon afterward, followed closely by his other relatives and friends.

The first seating was filled to capacity. As their guests left after dessert, others came in to take their place.

He wondered how many meals had been served so far. *Two hundred? Three hundred? More?* His mother looked pleased. He prayed that the amount raised would be enough to pay Joe's medical expenses.

"Jacob!"

"Rachel." With a smile, he approached his sister-in-law. "Need help?"

"*Ja*, there is more bread in Charlotte's kitchen. Would you mind getting five loaves?" She moved the breadbasket toward the front of the table.

Jacob nodded. "Do *ya* need anything else?"

"Nay." She glanced about the room. "Have you seen Noah?"

"He is outside with Arlin, helping him set up a table to sell his woodcrafts. Our uncle wants to help with Joe's expenses. He's suffered medical bills with our cousin Meg and appreciated the help he got from his community."

"That's kind of him." Rachel spied her husband and waved at him. She flashed Jacob a smile. "Keep Noah away from the dessert table. Tell him there is chocolate cake at home for him. I don't want him sampling the fund-raiser treats."

Jacob laughed. "I'll tell him and be right back with the bread."

Rachel smiled her thanks. Grinning, Jacob turned and stopped short. Annie Zook stood directly behind him with baskets of rolls, biscuits and muffins.

"Annie." She looked lovely in a light blue dress that matched her eyes, over which she wore a black apron. Silky tendrils of her golden hair peeked out from beneath her white prayer *kapp* and caught the light. Her smile reached her bright blue eyes. Her pink lips and pretty nose were exquisitely formed. *A glorious vision from God.*

Startled by his thoughts, he said, "I have to get bread." Then he excused himself and left. He stopped once briefly to speak with Noah before he headed toward Charlotte Peachy's kitchen.

Except when he helped carry items to the food table, Jacob seemed to avoid her, she noticed. When it came time for him to eat dinner, he chose to sit in his sister-in-law's area, a fact that bothered her greatly. She thought they were friends. At times, he talked and teased her, but on other occasions, he would eye her with a strange look that was disconcerting.

She watched from a distance as he smiled and laughed, at ease while talking with Rachel. Eli Lapp entered the room and approached his twin. Eli saw her and grinned. Her heart lightened as she waved at him.

"Annie!" *Mam* called her from the kitchen doorway, just a few feet away. "We're almost done," she said. "Did you eat?" Annie shook her head. "Well, get something, daughter. You've been working hard. You need to eat, and not only from the dessert table."

"Ja, Mam," she said without argument.

Toward the end of the evening, Charlotte Peachy approached. "We've done well." She beamed. "Almost four-thousand dollars!"

Arlin Hostetler, Katie Lapp's brother, entered the barn behind Charlotte. "And I sold over eight hundred dollars worth of merchandise," he said with a grin. He turned the money over to Charlotte.

"Nearly five thousand dollars in all," Charlotte corrected.

Annie blinked back tears. *"Danki.* You don't know how much this means to us."

"I think I do," Arlin said.

Annie sniffled and wiped her eyes. "What would we do without all of you?"

Mam approached. "How much did we make?" she asked, and Charlotte told her. "Thanks be to God!" Her eyes filled with tears.

"Let's clean up," Charlotte said. "I'll give this cash to Abram to lock up until tomorrow."

Annie, her mother and all who had helped to set up or serve pitched in to clean up afterward. When they were done, after the women promised to gather and discuss a future Saturday breakfast fund-raiser, families left for home.

"We did well at the fund-raiser today." Annie felt pleased that the breakfast had been such a success.

"*Ja,*" her *mam* said, "the money will be a good payment toward the hospital bills."

Annie murmured her agreement. Perhaps now her father would feel less stressed about the state of their finances, she thought with relief.

Saturday morning Annie started her chores. She did the wash and hung it on the clothesline with Barbara's help. The day was sunny but a bit cooler than it had been yesterday.

"There's a nice breeze," Annie said.

"*Ja*, the clothes will dry in no time." Barbara reached into the wicker basket and withdrew one of Peter's shirts. She fastened the bottom hem on the line with wooden clothespins. "Have you decided what to make for supper?" she asked casually.

"*Ja*, meat loaf, mashed potatoes and peas." Annie picked up a wet pillowcase and shook the wrinkles from it before pinning it into place. "I'm thinking cherry cobbler for dessert."

Barbara was quiet for a few moments as she continued to hang the damp garments. "Do *ya* think that's *gut* enough?" she asked.

"For Levi?" Annie frowned. "Barbara, the preacher has been coming to our house for dinner once a week for months. He always likes what we fix. Why should tonight be any different?"

Barbara secured a lavender dress to the clothesline

and then faced her sister. "I just thought we could do something special for him."

"Any particular reason?" Annie asked.

"Nay," she murmured. "I just thought, since he is a preacher…"

"Levi would be the first to tell you that he is no different than the rest of us." Annie sighed. "Stop worrying, Barbara."

Later, as she worked to fix the cherry cobbler, Annie grew thoughtful. *Is Barbara right?* She stirred the cherries until they were coated with sugar. Should she be fixing something special for the preacher? She frowned as she dumped the fruit into a large baking pan. *Nay, he always likes what I fix.*

Next, she worked to prepare the crumb topping made with cinnamon, sugar and dry oatmeal, which she sprinkled over the cherries and dotted with dabs of butter.

She'd have to watch Levi this evening to see if he was enjoying the food or just being polite. Annie picked up the cobbler pan and put it in the refrigerator.

Preacher Levi Stoltzfus was an honest man. He wouldn't come to supper every week if he didn't enjoy the food, she realized. She smiled. Just as she had told Barbara, there was no cause to worry that Levi wouldn't enjoy the meal. Levi Stoltzfus was a kind older man, who would make someone a good husband. He came to dinner often because he'd lost his wife in childbirth two years ago.

She went still. Were Barbara and *Mam* trying to play matchmaker? Was that why Barbara was worried about whether or not Levi enjoyed tonight's meal?

Annie laughed softly, scolding herself for her silly concern. *Mam* hadn't said a word about Levi, and the preacher was a frequent visitor so his visit was nothing out of the ordinary.

Nay, she thought. Barbara was just being Barbara, worrying about something for no reason.

Preacher Levi would make me a fine husband... He'd be kind to me, treat me fairly and I would never have to worry about him breaking my heart.

Unbidden came thoughts of Jacob Lapp with his twinkling golden eyes and warm smile, and Preacher Levi was temporarily forgotten.

Chapter Eight

Annie was at the stove, stirring potatoes, when she heard her sister's voice in the front room.

"Preacher Levi!"

"*Hallo*, Barbara. 'Tis nice to see *ya* again," he replied pleasantly. Seconds later, they were in the doorway.

"Levi," her sister said with warmth. "Are you hungry? We're having meat loaf for dinner."

"It smells wonderful." He entered the room behind Barbara.

Annie turned. "*Hallo*, Levi," she said with a smile. "Dinner is nearly ready. We'll be having mashed potatoes, buttered baby peas and fresh yeast rolls with the meat loaf." She grabbed the pot from the stove, set it on a hot mat on the countertop and reached for the butter. "What would you like to drink?"

"I'll get it," Barbara piped up. "Iced or hot tea? Lemonade? Coffee?"

"Iced tea would be fine." He flashed Annie an amused glance as Barbara hurried to retrieve the pitcher from the refrigerator in the back room. She raced back into the kitchen where she withdrew two glasses from a cabinet. She filled one to the brim with tea and handed it to Levi.

Mam entered the kitchen. "*Hallo*, Levi."

"Miriam." He smiled. "I appreciate the standing dinner invitation."

"'Tis always a pleasure to have you, isn't it, girls?"

Annie agreed while Barbara nodded.

"Where's Joe?" Levi asked.

"In the gathering room," Annie said. "Would *ya* mind telling him that it's time to eat?"

"I'd be happy to." As the minister left to visit with their father, Barbara turned toward her and exclaimed, "Why did you ask him to tell *Dat*? He shouldn't have to do anything. He's our guest."

Annie sighed. "Barbara, Levi wanted to see *Dat*— couldn't *ya* tell? And he is more like family than a guest." After stirring the potatoes, she drained the liquid from the pot into the sink and grabbed the masher.

Barbara looked taken aback. "But he's the preacher!"

"And you and I are Joe and Miriam's daughters. Does that make us any less in the Lord's eyes?" She worked the potatoes into a fine mash, added butter, milk and seasonings. "Barbara, would you please put the peas on the table? And maybe some jam as well as butter."

Soon supper was served and Annie called everyone to come and eat.

"Your *vadder* and Levi will be right in," *Mam* said. "I'm going to get your *grosseldre*."

"What's for dinner?" Peter asked as he passed his mother and entered the room. Annie gestured toward the table. "Meat loaf!" he cried, sounding pleased.

Josiah came in behind him and reached down to snag a piece of bread. "Looks *gut*."

"Josiah!" Barbara scolded. "Save some for supper."

Josiah gave her a look. "This *is* supper time, sister."

"Smells wonderful," Levi said as he pushed *Dat* into the room and into position at the table.

Soon *Mam* had returned with Annie's grandparents, and everyone was seated and ready to eat. The meat loaf was passed around, followed by the vegetables and bread.

"Levi." *Mam* handed him the dish of peas. "How long has it been since Rebecca passed on?"

Annie heard her sister gasp from beside her.

"Two years," Levi murmured.

"It must get lonely in that big house of yours." *Mam* smiled as she spooned mashed potatoes onto her plate.

"*Ja*, it can be," the preacher admitted.

Annie frowned. Levi had lost his wife in childbirth along with their baby. The preacher had no family left in Happiness. His parents had passed away ten years ago, leaving Levi and his five siblings. His two sisters had married and moved with their husbands to Indiana, while his eldest brother had died three years after their mother and father. Not long afterward, Levi's two living brothers had left Happiness and followed his sisters to Indiana.

Levi hadn't minded when his family moved away, for he had met and happily married Rebecca Troyer. Rebecca and Levi had wanted children, and at first it seemed that it wasn't meant to be. After five years of marriage, Rebecca and Levi had rejoiced that they were finally to have a child. Only it had all gone wrong, and Rebecca, who had suffered a difficult pregnancy, had endured a childbirth that had taken her life and their baby's.

Much to Annie's relief, her father changed the subject and asked Levi about the preacher's corn harvest.

Levi smiled. "*Ja*, it has been a *gut* year. The weather was fine for us. Now we have to think of next year. I was thinking of trying to plant some..."

The conversation turned to farming and from farming to this visiting Sunday.

"You will come tomorrow, won't you, Levi?" Barbara asked.

"With all the fine food you provide? *Ja*, I'll come." Levi had finished his plate and taken seconds. *Mam* rose to remove his dish when he was done.

"Annie made chocolate cake and cherry cobbler," *Mam* said as she carried the dessert to the table.

Levi smiled at Annie. "They both sound wonderful, but I'd like a piece of cherry cobbler."

"Annie is a *gut* cook, Levi. She will make some man a wonderful wife." *Mam* continued to extol Annie's talents, causing Annie's face to redden.

"Mam—"

"'Tis true, Annie," *Mam* said.

"Ja, you do cook well," Levi told her gently.

"She will make a fine wife, *ja*?" *Mam* asked.

Annie could feel the intensity of Levi's regard. *"Ja."* He appeared thoughtful, and she wished she could be anywhere but here at this moment.

"Miriam," *Dat* said, "you are embarrassing the girl, and you are forgetting your youngest daughter. Barbara is a fine cook, as well."

Annie was suddenly grateful that the attention had shifted to her sister, who didn't seem the least embarrassed by it. She frowned. *What is* Mam *doing?* She gasped. *Trying to make a match!* She closed her eyes. This wasn't the way to find a husband!

The preacher was a nice man, it was true, and he was attractive with his golden-blond hair and blue eyes. And she did feel comfortable around him, but something inside her rebelled at her mother's interference in matters of her heart.

Later that night, in her room, the memory of that moment mortified her. Levi Stoltzfus? Annie shook her head. She couldn't think of this now. She couldn't. Was her mother so determined to get her out of the house that she would push her toward Levi when the man wasn't ready to court or marry again?

"Annie?" Barbara's voice came out of the dark.

"Ja?" She stared up at the ceiling, not seeing anything but the images inside her head.

"Do you like him?"

"Who?" Annie rolled to face her.

"Preacher Levi."

"Ja, he is a nice man." He was more than a nice man, she thought, but she didn't want to be pushed into a relationship by her mother or her sister.

"Mam seems to think he should be for you."

Annie sighed. "That was obvious at dinner."

"What are you doing to do?"

She thought long and hard before answering. Levi would make her a fine husband, but he would have to be the one to show interest in her. "What can I do? 'Tis God's will that will decide."

Monday morning, Jacob was hanging up his hat in the shop when he heard a sound behind him.

"Jacob."

He spun, startled to see her. "Annie! You're here early."

"I couldn't sleep."

Jacob became concerned. Annie looked exhausted; there were dark circles beneath her eyes and a look of anxiety in her expression. His worry for her grew. "What's wrong? Is it Joe?"

She shook her head. "*Nay, Dat* is doing well. He goes back to the doctor this week."

"What's wrong, then?"

She blinked up at him, then looked away. "You'll think it's silly—"

"Something is worrying you, and I doubt it's silly."

She wandered about the room, running her fingers over the items on the worktable: a metal fire poker… different sizes of tongs and cross-peen hammers.

"Annie—"

"I think my *mudder* is trying to make me a match," she rushed to say.

"A match?" He stared at her. *With whom?* "You think she's trying to find you a sweetheart?"

"Sweetheart, *nay*." She stopped fidgeting to face him. "A husband."

"Your *mudder* wants to marry you off?" Jacob thought of other families within the community. It was possible. Not everyone was like his *mam* and *dat*, who had married for love and were happy to see their children discover the same happiness on their own.

"Preacher Levi comes to the house every week for supper," she began.

Jacob nodded. The preacher came to their house often, as well.

"The last time Levi ate with us, *Mam* suddenly mentioned his late wife and how long it had been since Rebecca had passed on—"

"Surely it was just an expression of concern for our preacher," he suggested as he reached for his leather apron. He slipped it over his head and tied it in the back at his waist.

Annie shook her head. "After reminding Levi how lonely he must be in his big house, *Mam* praised my cooking." She looked horrified, and he fought not to smile. "And then she told him what a wonderful wife I'd make." She blinked back tears. "It was humiliating."

"You said that you'd wanted to marry an older man." He gathered his tools and placed them within reach. "Levi is older. What's wrong with him?"

"There is nothing wrong with him," she said. "He's a kind man. Once he is over his late wife, I believe he will make someone a *wonderful* husband."

Jacob felt his heart skip a beat as she spoke. Levi Stoltzfus sounded like the perfect husband for her. "Then I would consider what you want and take your time to decide," he said.

"I could do that. It's not as if they will force me to marry him." Annie smiled and looked relieved. "That is sound advice. *Danki*, Jacob."

He nodded as he watched her closely.

Annie glanced about the shop. "I don't see any food in here. Would you like coffee and a cinnamon bun?"

"Ja." He grinned. "You are a fine cook, Annie Zook," he teased. "You'll make some man a wonderful wife one day."

She flashed him a look that told him she didn't mind his teasing. "I'll bring your coffee and roll." She suddenly looked mischievous. "Or I'll send Barbara out with hardboiled eggs and castor oil." She laughed as she left, and the sound of her laughter was like music to his heart.

Jacob felt a burning in his stomach. He didn't like the idea of Annie marrying Levi; he didn't like the idea of her marrying anyone but him. But if he had to pick an older husband for her, then Preacher Levi would be his choice.

He sighed. He seemed destined for heartbreak. He'd thought he could work in the shop and keep his emotions under control, but he'd lost that battle. He loved Annie. He wanted her for his wife. If being friends with her was his only choice, he'd take it. Friendship was better than having no relationship with her at all. But would he feel the same after she married someone else? Could he endure watching her with another man, holding his children? He wanted Annie to be happy and if her happiness meant her marriage to Levi Stoltzfus, then he would pray to the Lord to help him accept it.

Preacher Levi Stoltzfus wasn't the only man that *Mam* invited to take supper with the family. The following Wednesday, Joseph Byler arrived, much to Annie's surprise. Joseph was a young man who tended to be over-eager in everything he did. He was the son of Edna and the late John Byler. He was single, eighteen, and while he was attractive, he irritated Annie.

Joseph's presence, along with *Mam's* questions and comments regarding Annie's cooking skills, made Annie realize that Joseph was only the second in what could potentially be a long parade of prospective husbands invited by her mother.

Annie confronted *Mam* after Joseph went home. "What are *ya* doing?"

Her mother shrugged. "You promised to consider any man who showed an interest in you."

"But *Joseph Byler*? I can't possibly spend time with him. He is…*annoying.*"

Mam stared at her. "Annie!" she scolded.

Annie stood at the sink, drying the last of the supper dishes. "Would you want his attention?"

"He's a nice young man."

"*Ja*, too young. I want an *older* husband. I'll not accept him if he asks to court me. It wouldn't be fair to give him hope."

Her mother sighed, apparently accepting defeat. "I agree he can be overwhelming."

"Trying, you mean." Annie wrinkled her nose.

Mam gave her a look. "You need to think seriously about your future. If not Joseph, you must consider someone else." She paused. "What about Levi?"

"I'm not sure he's over his late wife."

"But you like him."

Annie nodded. "*Ja*. He is a kind man."

"There are other available men within our church community. All hope isn't gone yet," her mother assured her.

Annie raised her eyebrows. "I never thought it was." She frowned. "*Ya* think I'm so awful that no man would ask to court me on his own?"

"*Nay*, daughter. But you can't live in the past. You're getting older, and I'd like to see you settled with a husband and children."

"Miriam!" Joe called from the other room.

"Coming!" *Mam* touched her cheek. "Things will work out for the best, Annie. They always do." And she left Annie wiping the countertop, wondering what she would do if she didn't find a man with whom she could be content.

Levi Stoltzfus was definitely a better choice than Joseph Byler.

Please, Lord, give me the courage to accept Thy will and be happy.

The church community put on another fund-raiser for Horseshoe Joe, this one a breakfast. Jacob stood along one wall, looking for the best way to lend a hand. Today, the breakfast was to be held in the firehouse. Jed's boss, the firefighter who had arranged the use of tables and chairs for the dinner, had come to the bishop and offered the use of the large hall. Seeing the merit in the size of the room and the location, Bishop John accepted the offer. With the breakfast announced on the sign outside, Jacob knew the fund-raiser would be a success.

This morning the tables were lined with rolls of paper. It was 7:00 a.m., and soon people would arrive to eat.

Jacob saw his two sister-in-laws and Annie setting up. The cans of cooking fuel beneath the stainless-steel chafing dishes were lit and ready to go. His *mam*, Mae King and Miriam Zook were cooking scrambled eggs, pancakes, sausage, bacon and ham. Jacob made his way to the kitchen. The scents coming from the room were wonderful. They made his mouth water.

"Need any help?" he asked.

"Jacob! I'm glad you're here." His mother gestured toward a large metal pan on the worktable. "Would you take the sausage to the food table?"

"Ja, Mam." He lifted a metal lid to inspect the contents. He hadn't eaten yet this morning, and the delicious aroma wafting up from the breakfast sausage patties made his stomach rumble.

"When you're done with that, there'll be a dish of pancakes ready," Mae King asked.

"I'll be back soon." Jacob picked up the chafing dish and carried it out to the dining area. He passed Annie as he made his way out.

"Jacob," she said. "What do you have there?"

"Sausage." He enjoyed taking stock of her.

Her cheeks were flushed from rushing about, preparing for the event. "Rachel will tell you where to put it."

Jacob inclined his head. At the food table, he set the

full serving dish into a rack, as instructed, and as he headed back to the kitchen, he experienced an awareness of Annie across the room.

Annie watched Jacob chat briefly with Rachel before he set down the breakfast meat and left. With lingering mixed feelings, she scrutinized the food table. Everything was as it should be. She went to the kitchen and picked up the scrambled egg pan. She hurried toward the dining room and stumbled against Joseph Byler. "Joseph, you startled me!" she gasped, stepping back.

"Let me carry that for you," he said.

Annie kept a firm grip on the dish. "It's not heavy. I can manage."

"I insist." Joseph observed her with gleaming eyes as he started a tug-of-war with her over the metal pan.

Annie inhaled sharply and released it. "Take it to Rachel, please." She hurried back to the kitchen, eager to be away from the young man. "Are the pancakes ready?" she asked Mae as she entered the room.

"Ja." Mae wiped her hands on her cooking apron. "Dish is almost to the brim."

"I'll take these out to keep warm," Annie stated as she picked up the pan of pancakes. She hesitated then sighed. "Here comes Joseph Byler."

"He is a nice young man," *Mam* insisted.

"I'm not interested."

Joseph made a beeline in her direction as soon as he saw her. Annie managed a weak smile. "Next to the sausage," she instructed as she handed him the pan.

"I'll take care of it." He looked serious before he turned and left.

Annie watched him walk away, then sighing, she went to the drink table where she checked the large container of iced tea. She set out plastic cups and placed a hot mat where she would put out a thermal coffee decanter later. Another would be used for hot water for tea or hot chocolate. She eyed the area to decide what needed to be brought out now and what should wait until later.

As she turned, she saw Joseph Byler heading her way. She closed her eyes briefly and prayed. *Dear Lord, please grant me wisdom, patience and understanding so that I may deal kindly with Joseph Byler.* When she opened her eyes, Jacob Lapp was in her line of vision. She sent him a pleading look as she glanced pointedly toward Joseph. Jacob grinned and followed the young man as he approached.

"Annie, how else may I help?" Joseph asked.

"You can give Isaac and Eli a hand as they set up the last of the chairs." Jacob gestured toward the other side of the room. "I'll stay and help Annie."

Joseph opened his mouth as if to object, but then he nodded politely and left.

"May I carry something?" Jacob teased, his golden eyes twinkling.

Annie made a face at him and then laughed. "Would you like to?" she asked seriously.

"*Ja*, but I don't want to seem overeager like Joseph." Jacob glanced in the other man's direction.

"You're *not* Joseph," she said and felt her face heat. "I can use the help." She felt an odd sensation along her spine as he took her measure.

"What do *ya* want me to do?" he asked.

"We have several more food dishes in the kitchen. You can help me carry them out to the dining room." She examined the buffet tables. "More breakfast meat," she decided. "And fried eggs, if they're ready."

"Lead the way, Annie, and I will be happy to carry them for you."

Annie felt a tingling at her nape, overly aware of his strong presence behind her, as she preceded him into the kitchen.

"Back so soon?" Mae King asked.

"Came for the fried eggs," he said. He picked up the large metal dish.

"*Mam*, are there more muffins and sweet rolls?" Annie asked.

"*Ja*, in the backroom."

Katie wiped her hands on her cooking apron as she moved from the stove. "After you take those out, Jacob, would you help Annie by carrying the jams and jellies for the breadbaskets?"

"*Ja, Mam*. Anything else?"

"You can make sure the girl eats breakfast before we open the doors to our guests," Mae said.

Annie felt the warmth of Jacob's regard. "I will," he promised, and Annie looked into his twinkling golden eyes and blushed before she quickly headed into the other room for the breadbaskets.

"I don't see Joseph," Jacob said a short time afterward as they reentered the large dining area together. "Would *ya* like me to find him for you?"

Halting, Annie shot him a look. "Not funny." He shrugged and then chuckled. She responded to his good humor and joined in the laughter. "Come, Jacob, we need to put these on the other buffet table."

"May I sneak a muffin?" he said as he set down the jam and jelly tray next to the two large baskets that Annie had carried in. "I haven't eaten breakfast."

"You're not sneaking if you ask permission," she teased.

"*Gut* point." He snatched a chocolate-chip muffin and glanced about slyly, then took a small bite. He looked so comical that Annie grinned.

"Well?" she said. "Is it worth getting in trouble over?"

He feigned a frown. She couldn't miss the amusement in his golden eyes. "Am I in trouble?"

She smirked. "You *are* trouble." And as they shared laughter, Annie found great enjoyment in his company. As she turned to head back to the kitchen, she caught sight of her sister standing several feet away, staring at them. She met Barbara's glance and, to her dismay, watched as her sibling made an about-face and rushed toward the kitchen.

"*Ach, nay,*" Annie murmured.

"What's wrong?" Jacob asked, moving to her side.

"I'm afraid you'll be in the hot seat next. My sister saw us laughing, and now she's run to tell my *mudder*." She paused, gave him a worried look. "Be careful or you'll find yourself invited to dinner."

"Not a chance." Jacob glanced toward the kitchen doorway. "Your *mam* doesn't consider me as a potential husband for you. I have no job and no prospects." He smiled slightly. "See? So there's no need to worry. Just remind her that I'm too young for you."

Annie tilted her head at him. "Too young?" she murmured.

"*Ja*, I'm not your type at all, an older member of our church community." He grinned. "Coming?" He gestured toward the kitchen, and she inclined her head.

Annie followed slowly as Jacob went on ahead. *He's right*, she thought. That was exactly what *Mam* would think—that he was a young man without means. And

Jacob was everything she wanted to avoid in a man. She closed her eyes, felt a rush of pain. Why did she suddenly feel so sad?

Chapter Nine

Annie was in the yard, feeding chickens, when Jacob exited the shop and approached. "*Gut* morning!" she greeted with a smile.

"*Gut* morning. You are out early." He reached her side, dipped his fingers into her bucket and scattered a handful of feed.

She was conscious of him beside her, looking handsome in his maroon shirt and *triblend*-denim trousers. "*Mam's* gone into town with *Dat*. He has a doctor's appointment. Barbara and Josiah left for the Amos Kings' earlier this morning." She smiled. "Me? I've got a full day's chores." She threw another fistful. "You?"

"Ike King is bringing in his gelding. When I'm done in the shop, I'll head to Noah's." He captured her glance, causing warmth to rise up from her nape. "Jed is out with a construction crew, and Noah needs help with deliveries."

Annie broke eye contact with him until she could regain her balance. "What time will Ike be here?" She knew that Noah Lapp's furniture shop did well. Noah was an excellent cabinetmaker and the demand for his work had increased since he'd opened his business.

"Any minute now. I've come to watch for him."

"Do you have time for coffee?" she asked.

"*Nay*, but I appreciate the offer."

A buggy on the dirt drive drew Annie's attention. Beside her, Jacob called out a greeting and waved to Ike, who drove the vehicle.

Ike parked his buggy close to the shop entrance. He smiled as he climbed out. "Mornin'!" he greeted. "Fine day today." He was a man in his late thirties with a beard along his jawline. All Amish men grew beards after they married. Only Ike was a widower.

"Great weather to be out and about," Jacob agreed as he walked toward the horse and rubbed the gelding's nose. "I don't imagine we'll see many days like this before the cold rushes in."

The older man nodded. Studying him, Annie knew that Ike had left Indiana and returned home to Lancaster County after his young wife's death. Ike resembled his older brother Amos about the eyes and in the shape of his chin, but Amos's beard had streaks of gray while Ike's was reddish brown.

"Where do you want him?" Ike asked Jacob, referring to the animal.

"Inside." Jacob worked to help Ike unhitch the horse and then he instructed the other man to follow him into the blacksmith shop. "See you later, Annie."

"*Ja*, Jacob." She smiled at Ike, who didn't immediately follow. "Are you waiting? You can come in for coffee or tea."

"That is kind of *ya*, Annie, but Amos is coming to fetch me. I'll be back later when Jacob has finished shoeing young Abraham here."

"*Gut* day to *ya* then, Ike. I must get back to work. I'll see you on Sunday." Annie watched him as he joined

Jacob, and the two men stood outside the shop, talking for a time.

"Annie!" Levi Stoltzfus approached from the direction of her grandparents' house, drawing her attention. The handsome preacher wore a spring-green shirt, black suspenders and black pants.

"Levi!" Annie grinned as he drew near. "I didn't expect to see you today."

"I thought I'd stop and visit with your *grosseldre* this morning." He appeared pleased as he reached her side.

"I'm sure they appreciated the company." Annie regarded him with warmth. "*Mam* sees the changes in them as they age, and since *Grossmudder's* last illness and hospital stay, she worries about them."

The preacher nodded. "*Ja.* They seem to be getting around well now, though." He took off his black-banded straw hat and held it in his hands.

"*Ja*, thank the Lord." Annie scattered the last of the chicken feed, then chatted with Levi about the weather, the farm and the upcoming winter.

"I should be getting back," Levi finally said. "I've got chores to do."

"As do I." A warm breeze stirred the air, and Annie closed her eyes, enjoying the sensation. She heard a sharp inhalation of breath, and she quickly opened her eyes to catch an odd look on Levi's face.

"Annie, before I go…" He suddenly looked uncomfortable. "I was wondering—"

Annie regarded him with concern. "Is something wrong, Levi?"

"*Nay.*" His expression cleared. "I… Would you consider going for a buggy ride?"

She felt her breath hitch. "You want me to go for a ride with you?"

He nodded, looking very much like a young school-boy. "I'll understand if you—"

"I'd like that," she said hurriedly, and the idea of spending time with Levi seemed a sudden answer to her prayers. Jacob had told her to consider what she wanted. She wanted an older husband like Levi. Didn't she?

"Friday evening, then?" he said. "Or do *ya* have plans?"

Annie smiled as she shook his head. "*Nay.* Friday would be fine."

Levi looked relieved and genuinely happy. Annie felt a moment's doubt but pushed it away.

"We can talk about it tomorrow night," he said.

"So, you still plan to come to dinner?" she teased.

"I wouldn't miss your cooking, Annie," he said seriously.

"Roast beef?" Annie noted his expression and felt only slightly uneasy. The feeling passed as she reminded herself that this was Levi Stoltzfus, a man who had been coming to dinner every week for months.

"*Ja.* Sounds delicious." He put on his hat. "I will see *ya* tomorrow, Annie."

She had always felt at ease in Levi's presence. Why should that change just because he wanted to take her for a buggy ride? Because he realized that he liked her? She smiled and waved as he walked away. Annie turned toward the barn and saw Jacob Lapp standing near the shop entrance. Jacob gave her a look that made her feel uncomfortable before he and Ike disappeared into the shop.

Heart thumping hard, she hurried to store the feed, then shooed the chickens into a fenced area and secured the gate. With thoughts of Jacob and Levi swirling in her mind, Annie headed toward her grandparents' house. She had work to do.

As she approached, she spied her grandmother in the yard, watching a robin.

"It won't be long before they'll be gone for the winter," she said of the bird. "*Grossmudder*, did you and *Grossdaddi* have breakfast?"

"*Nay*, I wasn't hungry earlier."

"You had a visitor," Annie said. "Preacher Levi."

Grossmudder nodded. "*Ja*, he is a *gut* boy, that Levi." She fixed Annie with a look. "A fine preacher. He would be perfect for you."

Annie laughed, although her heart wasn't in it. She couldn't forget the strange look Jacob had given her. Why should he disapprove?

Her sister was back when Annie returned home. "You weren't gone long."

"*Nay,*" Barbara said. "I'd planned to do the laundry, but I see you already put in a load." She tightened the strings of her white apron, making sure the cape was neatly tucked inside.

"Is Josiah back?"

"*Ja*, he is in the barn seeing to the horses."

"Would *ya* help hang the sheets to dry? I put them on before I went over to *Grossmudder's*."

"*Ja*, I'll be glad to help. 'Tis too nice a day to be indoors."

"I'll meet *ya* outside," Annie said. She gathered the clothes from the propane washing machine and set them in the laundry basket. Then she headed outside and saw Barbara hanging the clothespin bag on the line within easy reach. Annie set down the clothes.

Barbara reached in to grab a sheet while Annie hurried to catch hold of the other end. With a snap of the wet fabric between them, they pinned the fabric on the line and then reached down for another.

"How are the Kings?" Annie asked conversationally.

"They are well. While I was there, Amos's brother Ike came to visit."

Annie secured a pillowcase. "Ike was here, too. Jacob made shoes for one of his horses this morning."

"Ike is a nice man," Barbara commented.

Annie reached up to swat away a bug. "*Ja*, he is pleasant."

"He is a widower," Barbara said casually.

"*Ja*, I heard." Annie fastened a bath towel to the clothes rope.

Barbara pulled a white prayer *kapp* from the basket, pegged it to the line by its strings. "He would make a *gut* husband."

"*Ja*." Annie smiled. "Are *ya* interested?"

"Me?" Barbara looked stunned. "*Nay*, I'm thinking of you."

Annie stared at her. "Why would *ya* think that Ike and I should be man and wife?"

"*Ya* want an older man, don't *ya*?"

Annie frowned. "How do you know that?" Had Jacob said something to Barbara? She felt a burning in her stomach.

"*Mam* told me," Barbara said. "It is a *gut* plan, Annie."

Annie was aghast. "You didn't say anything to Ike, did you?"

"*Nay*. I would not do that."

Relieved, Annie continued to hang clothes. "Thanks be to God," she murmured beneath her breath. To her sister, she said, "You don't need to be looking for a husband for me. It will happen in the Lord's time." She hesitated, then confided, "Levi has asked me to go for a buggy ride with him."

"I see." Barbara hung up a blue dress. "Then you like him."

"He is a *gut* man." Annie wondered if she was trying to convince herself.

"'Tis true." Barbara handed her one end of a sheet, and the sisters worked together to secure it on the line.

As they hung the laundry, Annie noticed that her sister had become suddenly quiet. "Barbara, is everything all right?"

Barbara looked at her and nodded. *"Ja."* Her smile didn't reach her eyes. "Come. We have a lot to do yet."

Later, as she prepared supper in the kitchen with her mother and sister, Annie wondered about her sister's sudden change in behavior. Why? Because of Levi's invitation to go for a buggy ride? Barbara had made a big fuss over Levi the last time he'd come to dinner. Was Barbara sweet on Levi? If so, what should she do about her outing with the preacher? She couldn't back out now. Could she?

Annie was thoughtful as she took the ham, green beans and potatoes out of the oven. She'd think of something. She didn't want to hurt her sister.

"Annie," a masculine voice said.

"Reuben!" She smiled. "Come in and sit. Where's your sister?"

Reuben hesitated. "She didn't come."

"How is Rebekkah?" Barbara asked as she entered the room. She didn't seem surprised to discover him there.

"She is *fine*. She is with our *grossmudder* this evening."

"Is she all right—your *grossmudder*? The rest of the

family?" Annie asked. "It's been a while since we've seen all of you."

He nodded. "It's been months, and *ja*, they are all doing well."

"You are just in time." Annie pulled the tray of yeast rolls out of the oven and turned with a smile. "I hope you brought your appetite." She set the tray on pot holders on the countertop.

"Reuben." *Dat* entered the kitchen on crutches. Annie automatically pulled out a chair for him, and he maneuvered himself to the table and sat down. Peter, Josiah and the *grosseldre* came to the table.

"I heard about your accident, Joe." Reuben eyed her *dat* with concern. "It looks like you're getting around."

"*Ja*, although my progress is slower than I'd like it to be."

"Things will improve, and soon it will be just a story to tell your grandchildren." Reuben accepted his plate from Barbara, who had added meat, potatoes and succotash. "My *vadder* does well after his injury."

Annie saw her *dat* nod. "That must have been bad, injuring himself in the corn binder."

Reuben agreed. "I was just a boy at the time, but I'll never forget how tore up his arm was. He nearly lost it. The doctors at the hospital were able to do surgery and now years later *Dat* has *gut* use of the arm."

Annie thought of Reuben's father and recalled his scarred arm. It was a blessing that Jonas Miller was left-handed. Still, his concern over how he would manage long term must have been worrisome to him.

"The Lord gives us the strength to handle what we must and the courage to continue in times of great worry," Annie said.

"Amen," *Mam* murmured with a quick glance at

her parents. Suddenly, she grinned. "Everyone hungry?" she asked as she ensured that everyone—the men especially—had their food.

After saying a prayer of thanks, they ate and talked and ate some more. In preparation for dessert, Annie stood and collected the dinner plates.

"I heard Rebekkah is seeing someone," *Mam* said.

"Ja," Reuben said. "She's being courted by Caleb Yoder. They plan to marry, and the banns will be posted this Sunday."

"How wonderful!" *Mam* exclaimed. After a short pause, she'd then asked, "And you? Are you courting anyone?"

"Nay. I haven't found the right woman yet."

Mam had risen from the table, gone to the counter and picked up a rich chocolate cake. "You should try a piece of cake." She'd set it in the center of the table. "Annie made it."

Later that night, Annie lay in bed and felt her face redden at the memory of dinner with Reuben. She should tell Jacob. He'd put things into perspective for her. *Ja*, she would tell Jacob of her mother's latest matchmaking attempt and see what he had to say.

But first she had to tell her mother about Levi wanting to take her for a buggy ride with him, and her dilemma with Barbara. Unless… Annie began to think, and came up with an idea.

"Reuben!" Annie was surprised to see him again so soon. "What are *ya* doing here?"

"Hallo, Annie. I wanted to stop by and ask if you are going to the next church Sunday singing."

"I thought I might." Annie stepped off her front porch,

carrying a laundry basket of clothes. She headed to the clothesline, dismayed when Reuben followed her.

"Will you consider allowing me to take *ya* home afterward?"

Annie set down her basket and stood. "That is nice of you, Reuben, but that's over a week away. I'm not sure of my plans yet, and I wouldn't want to hold you up."

He nodded, and to her relief, he didn't seem disappointed. "We'll see what happens during the next week. I know 'tis been a while since I came to a singing in your church district. I had a *gut* time when I did." He smiled. Fair-haired and with blue eyes, Reuben Miller was a handsome young man. *Not as handsome as the Lapp brothers*, she thought and then mentally scolded herself. She reminded herself how she wanted to steer clear of attractive men who could break her heart.

"It was a wonderful supper last night, Annie."

Annie bent to pull a green shirt out of the clothes basket. "I'm glad you enjoyed it," she said as she pinned it into place.

"I especially liked the chocolate cake," he said.

"That's of kind of you to say." She continued to hang clothes, hoping that he would decide that he should take his leave and return home. "You've got a free day today?" she asked conversationally as she hung a pair of one of her brother's pants.

"*Nay.* I brought my *dat's* mare for new shoes. Jacob said he could fit her in today."

Annie blinked. "Is she inside already?" Jacob was already here? She hadn't seen him come.

"*Ja*, he's in the shop. He said to arrive early, that he could take Aggie, and so here I am."

Annie was thoughtful, her mind racing with visions of Jacob shoeing the Millers' horse. He was *gut* at the work, just as her father had said he would be. Business had increased since Jacob had come to help in the blacksmithy. With the cooling weather of late autumn, he was bound to be busier than normal as folks brought their animals in for shoes before the onset of winter. She had wanted to talk with him, tell him about last evening, but she doubted he'd have any time for her.

"Annie."

She was startled. *"Ja?"* She blushed, realizing that Reuben must have called her name several times before she'd heard him.

"Did *ya* want coffee while *ya* wait?" she asked politely. "I can bring it to the shop." Then she would have a chance to see Jacob and bring him a cup, as well.

"Nay, I'm not much of a coffee drinker."

"Tea, then?"

He moved in too closely, and she shifted away as she continued to hang clothes. *"Nay,"* he said after a brief moment of hesitation. "I'll be heading back to the shop. Jacob's almost done with Aggie. You have a nice day."

Relieved, Annie gave him a genuine smile. "You, too, Reuben." He hadn't mentioned the singing again, and Annie was grateful.

By the time she'd hung all the clothes on the line, Annie saw Reuben leave the shop, leading his father's mare. Her heart gave a thump as Jacob exited the building behind him. She watched them talk a moment before Reuben hitched Aggie on to his buggy. He looked over, saw her watching him and waved before he climbed into the vehicle.

Jacob had briefly gone back into the shop, returning outside in time to see Reuben's wave. Jacob stared at her, and she felt suddenly awkward. She had yet to tell him about her conversation with Levi or about Reuben's presence at dinner last night. She studied Jacob for a long moment while trying to decide if she should approach him now or talk with him later. He took the decision out of her hands when he reentered the shop without a wave or a smile.

Annie fought the urge to cry. *You've got work to do, Annie*, she told herself, trying her best to put Jacob from her mind. He was probably too busy. He didn't have time to talk, not with the increase in work.

As she crossed the yard and climbed the front porch, she heard the approach of another vehicle, a wagon with a team of two horses. Jacob would most definitely be busy today, she realized, and she took heart that he wasn't ignoring her. His mind was simply focused on business matters.

Chapter Ten

Friday evening, Levi arrived in his open courting buggy. He came to the door, and her mother let him in. "I've come for Annie," he said.

"I'm here," Annie announced as she came from the back of the house, and the two went outside. It was a pleasant and clear evening. Annie had told her mother about the buggy ride once the preacher had left after his usual supper visit. Her mother hadn't said much, but the happy gleam in her eyes had spoken volumes.

Mam stepped out onto the porch as Levi helped Annie into the vehicle. Barbara came out and approached cautiously. Seconds later, Levi assisted Barbara, who looked embarrassed as she climbed up. "*Mam* says I'm to be your chaperone," she said solemnly as Levi got in. "Peter wanted to go, but—"

"'Tis fine, Barbara," Annie interrupted before her sister could say more. She had made the suggestion to *Mam* that Barbara come with them.

Levi nodded as if he understood. Preacher or not, they were not betrothed and needed someone to accompany the two of them. He smiled at her as he reached for the reins. "Where shall we go?"

"Wherever you wish," Annie said softly.

With a click of his tongue, he flicked the reins and drove the horse out onto the paved main road. Annie sat back, prepared to enjoy the ride.

Monday morning Joe sat in his wheelchair, watching as the younger man put shoes on Janey, one of the Lapps' horses. "You're doing well, Jacob. I am grateful for all the work you've done for me and my family."

Jacob stopped and flashed Joe a glance. "I've not done anything another man wouldn't have done."

"*Nay*, son," Joe insisted. "No one else has the skill or the knowledge."

Jacob had been surprised to see the older man wheel himself inside the shop earlier this morning. Horseshoe Joe had been getting around with a wooden crutch with his leg brace. Joe's leg must be causing him great pain, he thought with sympathy.

"'Tis nothing," Jacob said. "I've enjoyed the work. I was always fascinated watching you when I was younger." The horse shifted restlessly, and Jacob took a moment to soothe the animal. The sound of his familiar voice did the trick, and the mare settled.

Jacob carefully worked on Janey's right front foot, removing the old shoe and then preparing her hoof before he picked up the new one to compare it with the other. After examining them, he was satisfied with the result. He lifted the animal's hoof, set the shoe and then carefully nailed it into place.

"There you go, girl," he murmured before he started the same process on the left side.

Joe was unusually quiet as Jacob worked. Jacob paused. "Joe, are *you* all right? I can take you back to the *haus*."

The older man smiled. "I'm fine, Jake. Just a bit tired is all. My eldest stopped in to visit last night."

Jacob raised an eyebrow. "Joan?"

Joe nodded, his expression softening. "Haven't seen her, Adam or the *kinner* in months. It was *gut* to see them."

"Are they still here?" Jacob asked as he went back to the task at hand.

"*Nay.* They stayed the night and left early this morning. They're traveling to Delaware, said they wanted to stop and see us before they moved on. They plan to return for a longer visit on their way back."

Jacob smiled as, after finishing the front hooves, he returned to double-check each shoe on Janey's rear hooves. He had replaced them over a month ago, his first attempt since he was a young boy. He'd been grateful that she'd belonged to his family; the animal's trust in him had allowed Jacob to get the job done. His success with the mare had given him the confidence to continue the work. After remembering to lean in to brace the animal, he found the job easier than he'd recalled.

"I'm going to put Janey outside, Joe," he said. "I'll be right back. Did *ya* need me to get you something from the *haus*?"

"Coffee would be *gut*."

Jacob smiled. "I could use a cup myself. I'll see if Miriam can put a pot on."

"If she's busy," Joe said, "ask Annie. She makes a *gut* cup of coffee."

Jacob felt a flutter within his chest at the mention of Annie. She did make a good cup of coffee. It had been some time since he'd spoken with her. The memory of her and Reuben, talking outside while Annie hung clothes, still stung. Reuben and Annie? He didn't believe Reuben was the right man for her.

"I'll be right back," he said as he led the animal toward the door.

"Ask Annie about her outing with the preacher," Joe called out as Jacob reached the door.

"Levi Stoltzfus?" he asked, experiencing discomfort.

"*Ja*, he came for her Friday evening. Can't say if she's seen him again, but he's due to come by for another meal next week."

Jacob felt his heart ache as he stepped out into the sunny autumn day and glanced toward the house. There was no sign of life outside. He tied Janey to a hitching post and then headed slowly toward the residence, his thoughts in a whirl. He knew Reuben had taken supper with the Zooks, but he hadn't known about Annie and Levi.

I shouldn't be surprised. I did see them talking together. Annie hadn't visited him in the shop lately. He had no idea what Annie was thinking or feeling, and it bothered him.

He went to the back entrance that led into the kitchen. The inside door was open, allowing in the fresh air through the screen. Soon, it would be too cold to enjoy raised windows and open doors. He could smell the delicious scent of baking. His mouth watered. He peered inside and saw Annie opening the oven. She reached in with pot holders and removed what looked to be a breakfast cake, then set it on top of the stove. He didn't want to startle her, so he waited a minute until she moved away from the stove. He lifted his hand and knocked softly.

She turned quickly, saw who it was and smiled. "Jacob! Come in, come in."

"*Hallo*, Annie. Your *vadder* wants coffee."

"Just made a fresh pot." She pulled out two cups and placed them on the counter, before she reached for the vessel on the stove.

Jacob came farther into the kitchen. He enjoyed what he saw. Everything about the room—the warmth and feeling of home, the aromas of fresh coffee, vanilla and cinnamon—spoke of Annie. He swallowed. He promised himself that he would protect his heart, but he'd failed. There were too many wonderful things about her to resist loving her.

He studied her back. The royal blue dress, which brightened her eyes, looked wonderful on her. She wore a cooking apron tied about her neck and waist. He noted the tiny tendrils of golden-blond hair at her nape. He noted every little thing about Horseshoe Joe's daughter. She turned and flashed him a smile that lit up her face. He felt his heart give a little jump before it picked up again at a faster pace.

"I've poured you a cup, as well," she said as she set two on the kitchen table.

He nodded his thanks. "How does your *vadder* like his coffee?"

"Black, lots of sugar. His is the one on the right."

Jacob reached to pull the cups closer. He saw with delight that she had fixed his just the way he preferred, just as she'd made it for him previously. He took a quick sip. As expected, it was delicious.

"Cake?" She placed a hot mat on the table and transferred a baking pan from the counter to the pad. "Fresh out of the oven. Cinnamon-streusel coffee cake."

He sniffed appreciatively. "It smells wonderful."

"I think you'll like it," she said with a smile. "Do you want some?"

He grinned. *"Ja."* He watched as she cut a piece. "And

make sure you have a slice for your *vadder*. I don't think he'll like watching me enjoy your cake without his own." He observed as she prepared two generous helpings.

"I'll take these out and come back for the rest." With cups in hand, he turned to leave.

"Jacob."

He halted and glanced back.

"I can carry this out for you. There is something I want to tell you—"

Peter entered the kitchen. "Cake! Can I have a piece?"

"Nay." Annie grinned to show that she was teasing and offered a piece to her brother.

"Hallo, Jake," the boy said as he spied him in the room. "'Tis *gut* to see *ya*. Is my *vadder* in the shop?"

"Ja, I'm heading back there now." Jacob smiled. He liked Annie's younger brother. He was a nice boy, who worked hard on his father's farm. "Annie." He nodded toward the plates Annie had wanted to carry for him. "I'll be back for those." She was busy. There was no need for her to come out to the shop. She opened her mouth as if to say something, glanced quickly at her brother and kept silent.

"I'll bring them out to the shop for you," Peter said.

"I'd appreciate it." Jacob flashed Annie one last glance, then left. As he headed back toward the shop, he was afraid he knew what Annie wished to tell him. About her outing with the preacher.

He couldn't fault Annie's choice; Levi Stoltzfus was a fine man. But he wasn't him. *He* wanted to be the one taking buggy rides with Annie. He forced a smile as he entered the shop. He couldn't let Joe see how upset he was. The idea of Annie with another man was painful to him.

"Joe," he greeted cheerfully as he stepped into the

shop, "I've brought your coffee. Peter is bringing us coffee cake."

"Did you visit with Annie?" Joe asked.

Jacob shook his head. "She was too busy to talk."

While she cleaned up the kitchen, Annie thought of Jacob. He'd seemed quiet…too quiet. What was wrong? Their conversation had begun friendly, then suddenly Jacob had seemed in a hurry to get back to the shop. She sighed. She wanted badly to tell him about Levi and Reuben, just as she had with all of the other men her mother had tried to match her with.

She'd done the right thing in asking Barbara to accompany her and Levi as their chaperone. Annie had been silent during the ride, while Levi and Barbara had kept up a steady stream of conversation. They had driven through the country roads, enjoying the scenery and the fall weather. She had observed the preacher with her sister, noting each time Barbara blushed at something Levi said. When the sun had begun to set, Levi had driven the buggy back to the farmhouse. Annie had climbed down from the vehicle and waited to talk with Levi after her sister was done chatting with him. Barbara had ended the conversation and looked sheepish as she passed Annie on her way toward the house.

Levi had approached, his brow furrowed. "Annie—"

"I know, Levi. You don't have to say it. I appreciated the ride, but I think you and my sister are better suited."

"You're not angry?" he asked, looking apologetic.

"*Nay*, why should I be angry? It was a buggy ride. If you like Barbara, ask her to go next time. If you don't," she said softly, "please keep your distance. I don't want my sister hurt."

"I would never hurt Barbara."

"Gut." Annie smiled. "Next time, *Mam* may ask Peter to be your chaperone," she warned.

Levi nodded and then glanced toward the house, where Barbara waited inside the screen door. "May I talk with her before I go?"

Annie had nodded. "I'll send her out."

Now, as she finished tidying the kitchen, her thoughts went to Jacob. She wanted to tell him about her mother's continued matchmaking attempts. She wanted to tell him about Levi and Barbara. She wrapped up some of the cinnamon-streusel cake to take to her grandparents. She thought of her daily chores and knew she had a lot to accomplish. She picked up a broom to sweep the floor and then headed into the gathering room. She heard the kitchen screen door slam against the side of the house.

"Annie!"

Annie returned to the kitchen. "Peter?" She saw his frightened face and felt her chest tighten. "What's happened? What's wrong?"

"'Tis Jacob! He burned himself!"

"How?" she asked. She saw the odd look on her brother's face as he glanced away and then down at his feet. "How bad?" she rephrased the question.

Peter lifted his head, looked at her. "Bad enough," he admitted. "The burn is on the back of his hand, and it's bright red."

Her heart kicked into high gear. "I'll bring ointment." Annie ran to the medicine cabinet for a tube of B & W Ointment. She returned to the kitchen to find that Peter had disappeared.

Annie paused to consider what else she needed in order to dress Jacob's burn. After grabbing a bowl, she ran to the back room freezer for ice, then hurried to the kitchen for water and a towel before she raced across the yard.

Hissing at the pain, Jacob examined the burn on his hand. "It's red and swelling." And it hurt like fire.

"It looks awful." Peter hovered nearby, alternately pacing and stopping to inspect Jacob's burn. "This is my fault," he cried.

"*Nay*, Peter, I was clumsy."

"But you wouldn't have taken off your gloves if not for me," Peter cried.

"Come away from the anvil, Jacob, and sit down over here," Joe urged. He gestured toward a chair near the worktable. "Annie is on her way. She'll know what to do to help you."

Jacob obeyed and took a seat. Water blisters were forming on the burn. He flexed his hand and hissed at the growing intensity of the nonstop fiery pain. He'd been careless, his thoughts on Annie with Levi Stoltzfus.

Annie burst into the shop, carrying several items. "Jacob! Let me see." Her prayer *kapp* was slightly askew on her head, no doubt the result of her wild dash across the yard. She still wore her quilted cooking apron, and he immediately detected the mingled scents of fresh cinnamon and pure vanilla as she drew near.

Jacob sat and extended his arm. The last thing he needed was for Annie to play nursemaid. He felt a tingling awareness when she took hold of his hand. "It looks worse than it is," he assured her.

"*Nay*, Jacob. You've got a second-degree burn. It is as bad as it looks." Annie studied him with concern. She suddenly took charge in a no-nonsense manner. "I've brought cold water and burn cream." She set a bowl on the table beside him. "Put your hand in this," she said. "More water than ice, but it will help numb the pain."

When he didn't immediately move, she gently took his wrist and eased his burned hand into the dish. Jacob inhaled sharply. The harsh chill felt good against his throbbing, tender skin. He shuddered. But it was the sensation of her fingers about his wrist that most affected him.

Her blue eyes filled with compassion. "I'm sorry," she said. "I know it hurts, but the water is *gut* for it. And it will help clean out the burn." She glanced down, made a sound of dismay and removed her cooking apron.

Jacob kept his hand submerged and watched her. His heart beat a wild tattoo at Annie's closeness. Her scent of home and baked goods was a heady combination for his lovesick heart.

Annie stood patiently while he soaked his hand. She then laid a clean tea towel on the worktable and reached to gently lift his hand from the bowl. "You should come up to the *haus*," she urged as she carefully placed his hand on the towel, palm side down, burn side up. "I can take better care of your injury there."

"I will be fine," he said gruffly.

"After I put on this ointment," she argued, "I'll need to cover the burn with gauze." She unscrewed the lid off the jar and dipped her finger into the B & W Ointment, which she spread gently over his blistered skin. "I'll need to bandage it."

"*Ja*, Jacob," Joe agreed. "You need to listen to Annie. Go with her up to the *haus* and get that hand taken care of properly. Peter will clean up here. You'll not be doing any more work for a while."

He didn't want to follow her, but he did—for Joe. Having Annie minister to him was bittersweet. As he strode behind her toward the house, Jacob observed her, enjoying the view. He saw the fine curve of her nape beneath the back of her prayer *kapp*, and with an aching heart, he looked away.

Annie waited for him to catch up, and then he walked beside her, aware of her frequent looks of concern.

She stopped at the door, opened it for him to enter. "Sit," she ordered as she moved across the kitchen. He tried not to appear startled when she crouched before him and took his hand. She examined it closely, turning it to inspect it from all angles. She rose to her feet. "I'll do what I can here, Jacob, but you may need to see a doctor."

"*Nay*, I'll—"

"*Ach*, don't you be arguing with me," she said as she washed her hands. Reaching into a cabinet, she withdrew a small box, which she set on the dining table. Millie padded into the room and pushed against her leg. "Not now, Millie. Go lie down," she commanded, and he saw the dog obey and curl up in the corner.

· Silently, he watched as Annie opened the box and removed a roll of medicine tape with two packages of sterile gauze.

"You seem to know what you're doing," he said as she pulled a chair close to his. She captured his hand and gently spread another layer of ointment over the burn. He inhaled sharply, disturbed by her touch.

She didn't seem to notice. Her eyes on his injury, she smiled crookedly. "You don't cook as often as I do without suffering a burn or two from the oven or stove."

She rose and went to the sink to clean the ointment from her fingers. "You must be careful to keep it clean," she instructed as she returned to her seat. "No farm or shop work—nothing that could cause infection in your wound."

She tore open the package of gauze and secured two

squares over the wound with the medical tape. He didn't seem to feel the pain as much in Annie's presence.

"I'll take you home," she said, startling him.

He stood abruptly. "I can drive."

She placed a hand on his arm, and he felt the warmth of her fingers through his broadcloth shirt. "*Nay*, your buggy is here, but *you* shouldn't be holding the reins. If you'd prefer, I'll walk to your house and ask one of your brothers to come drive *ya*. Or you can save time and allow me to do it. I'm sure someone there will be happy to bring me back."

"Annie—"

"Please, Jacob," she pleaded. "Let me see *you* home."

He groaned inwardly. The last thing he needed was to be close to Annie Zook in a closed buggy. "Fine. If you insist, then I will go with you."

She flashed him a radiant smile. "Stay here." She got up and pushed in her chair. "I'll tell *Dat*."

He grabbed his hat off the kitchen table. "I will come with you, since the wagon is parked near the shop."

She stared at him a long moment through narrowed eyes before she nodded. She was silent as he fell into step beside her. He kept quiet; he had nothing to say. As they reached the building, Jacob allowed her to precede him inside. He listened calmly while she explained to her father where she was going.

"I can take him," Peter offered.

"Nay," Joe said, surprising Jacob. "Your sister will drive him. I need you to help me with a few things here." He eyed Jacob with concern. "Watch that hand, Jake. Annie will bring you home. Think about seeing a doctor, *ja*?"

Jacob lifted his uninjured hand. "I will call one in the morning if the burn looks worse."

"Are *ya* ready?" Annie asked.

Jacob didn't want to ride with her, but what other choice did he have? "I will talk with you soon," he told Joe.

"Take care of that hand, Jacob." Joe followed in his wheelchair. Peter was silent as he exited the shop with his father.

Without thought, Jacob started to climb into the vehicle's left side. "*Nay*, Jacob," Annie scolded.

Embarrassed, he managed to grin. She flashed him a look of steel that had him skirting the vehicle to climb up on the other side. He used his good hand to grab hold and hoist himself onto the bench seat. Annie got in next to him and picked up the leathers.

"I'll be right back, *Dat*," she said.

"Take your time," her father told her. "Make sure Jacob is taken care of. We can manage without you for a while."

Annie looked momentarily startled, but then she smiled and waved as she turned the horse toward the road. Jacob was silent as she steered the horse down the dirt lane and onto the paved main road. The only sounds were the soft thud of each horse hoof and the noise of the metal wagon wheels rolling along.

"You drive well," he said, feeling the need to break the silence. When it was quiet, he was too consumed by thoughts of the woman beside him.

She didn't take her eyes off the way ahead. "Janey is a *gut* horse. Your family has had her a long time. She listens well."

"*Ja*." Struck silent by her smile, he turned toward the side window opening. "She is a fine animal, and we are glad to have her." Being this close to Annie made him realize how much he cared for her. He was conscious of her quiet strength, her warmth and her pleasing clean scent as she handled the reins. When she'd ministered to his wounded hand at the house earlier, he'd been close to confessing his feelings for her. But he'd kept silent. What would she say if he told her now? He wanted to hold on to this moment, when he almost could believe that she might care. He felt the strongest urge to face her, to touch her hair and tug teasingly on her *kapp* strings. She stirred something within him that urged him to discover a way to keep her in his life and by his side.

Chapter Eleven

As she steered the horse-drawn wagon toward the Lapp farm, Annie was anxiously aware of Jacob's silence. "Your hand hurts."

He appeared startled and then his expression turned wry. "*Ja*, it's throbbing. I'll live."

She turned her attention back to the road. "I'm sorry this happened." She hesitated. "Was it Peter's fault?"

"*Nay*. I became distracted."

"Peter says it's his fault."

"*Nay*, I took off my work glove before he accidentally knocked a table peg off the anvil. I didn't think, and I brushed the back of my hand against the hot metal as I leaned to pick it up."

"Table peg?" She flashed him another glance.

"*Ja*. Rick Martin bought a table from a used furniture dealer. The legs are secured with metal pegs. One was bent and another missing. Rick asked me to make replacements for him." He offered her a pain-filled smile. "It was my fault, not Peter's."

She looked skeptical. "You are a kind man, Jacob Lapp."

He was silent as he stared out of his side of the vehicle. "I don't feel kind."

She frowned. Not kind? She wanted to ask why he felt this way. He obviously didn't know himself well. He was thoughtful, generous and had a good heart. Annie steered the conversation in another direction to distract him from his pain. "I wanted to tell you earlier—before Peter came into the kitchen—Reuben Miller came to dinner the other night."

"I saw him talking with you in the yard," he said quietly.

"He said he came for new horseshoes." Annie waited for his response.

"*Ja*, he did," he said. "The job didn't take long. I replaced the mare's front shoes. Your *vadder* changed out the others last summer."

Annie gave him a look. "My *mudder's* been playing matchmaker again. Reuben was invited to the house as the next in line as my potential husband." She sighed. "I wish she would stop interfering."

"You don't like Reuben?" he asked.

"He is nice enough, but he isn't what I'm looking for."

"*Ja*, you want to marry a church elder."

Annie nodded but kept her eyes on the road ahead of her.

"Levi," he guessed.

"*Nay*," she murmured. "He likes Barbara."

"Barbara?" He sounded surprised. "I thought you went on an outing with him."

She nodded, surprised that he'd known. "*Ja*, I did, with Barbara as our chaperone." She smiled crookedly. "They had a wonderful time together. It was I who felt like the chaperone."

"I'm sorry," Jacob said.

Annie shrugged. "I'm not. There are other older men in our community."

"Why do you want only an older man?" Jacob asked. "Don't *ya* want someone who'll cherish you?"

She flashed him a look, startled by the intensity of his golden gaze. Cherish? She was hoping for someone who would simply be happy to have her to wife. She would feel blessed to be cherished by her husband, but she doubted that would ever happen.

"Younger men don't want me." Annie felt her face heat. "I can trust an older man."

"What about me?" Jacob asked.

"You?" She became flustered. "What about you?"

"Don't you trust me?"

"I trust you," she hedged, wondering where the conversation was leading. "We are friends—" He shifted in his seat and Annie saw him wince. "I'm sorry. Your hand is hurting you."

"I'm fine," he insisted, but his pale features said otherwise.

The Samuel Lapp farm was several yards ahead. Annie flipped on the buggy's battery-operated turn signal as the vehicle approached the dirt road. She waited for two cars to pass, then when the path was clear, she carefully steered the horse onto the lane that led to their farmhouse. She was glad that conversation had ended. She didn't know why he'd started it.

"I'll ask Eli to take you home," Jacob said as she parked in the barnyard.

"Danki." She glanced his way as he shifted to get out. "Jacob—"

He turned, his brow furrowed. "I'm fine, Annie."

She touched his arm, felt the muscle tighten. "I'm sorry this happened."

One corner of his mouth curved upward as he shrugged. "You don't have to apologize." He held up his bandaged hand. "You're not responsible."

"You will see a doctor?"

"I'll see how it is in the morning. If it looks worse, then, *ja*, I'll see a doctor."

She nodded, satisfied. It was all she could ask of him. "Until then, if you need anything—" She bit her lip. "You'll tell me?" She leaned closer and stared into his eyes. *"Please?"*

He stared back at her, his good hand cradling his injured one. Finally, he broke eye contact. "I'll get my brother Eli." He walked a few feet and then stopped and faced her. "Annie, you said you trust me. I want you to consider something carefully...*me*."

As Jacob headed toward the house again, Annie climbed out of the vehicle, skirted the buggy and waited outside in the yard. *Him?* Was Jacob actually suggesting that she consider him as someone who could be more than a friend? Had he been serious? Or just teasing her? Now that he had put the idea in her mind, she had trouble dismissing it. They were friends, she reminded herself. Then why did she feel flustered whenever Jacob was near?

She stared at the house, waiting for Eli. Within minutes, Katie Lapp appeared. "Annie!" Jacob's mother called out to her. "Come inside while you wait."

Annie smiled shyly as she climbed the porch steps and entered through the door Katie held open.

"I did the best I could for him," Annie said as she moved into the warmth of Katie's kitchen, "but you may want to check his hand yourself. I'm afraid he'll be stubborn about seeing a doctor."

"I'm sure you did fine, Annie, but if it makes you feel

better, I'll examine the burn later." Katie smiled at her as she gestured for Annie to sit down. "Our men can be stubborn creatures."

"*Ja*, and Jacob, I fear, is more stubborn than my *vadder*, who is stubborn as a mule." Annie gasped and covered her mouth, realizing what she'd said, but Jacob's mother chuckled. "I can walk home. 'Tis no trouble, and the day is pleasant outside."

Katie shook her head. "Eli will take you. Jacob went upstairs to get him."

"*Ach*, I don't want to impose."

Katie turned on the stove and put on a kettle. "Will *ya* have tea?"

Annie thought a moment. *Dat* had told her to take her time. "*Ja*, I'd like that."

"*Gut.*" As the water heated on the stove, Jacob's mother reached into the cabinet for cups.

Jacob and Eli entered the kitchen as their mother brewed the tea. "Annie is going to enjoy refreshments before you take her home, Eli. I made you each a cup."

"If *ya* don't mind, *Mam*, I would prefer something cold." Jacob held up his bandaged hand. Annie was conscious that he avoided her gaze. She wanted to pull him aside and ask him if he'd been teasing earlier about considering him as a potential husband instead of someone older.

"How about a root beer?" his mother asked.

"That would be *gut*." Jacob pulled out a chair and saw Eli smile at Annie as he took the seat next to her.

"*Hallo*, Annie," his twin said.

She smiled. "Eli. You have time to take me home?"

"*Ja*. After we enjoy our tea."

"Annie." Katie handed Annie a cup and then extended one toward Eli.

After accepting it from her, Eli prepared the tea the way he liked it. "How is Joe?" he asked.

"*Dat* is fine. Doing better." Annie frowned as she watched Jacob. She had noticed that he'd winced a time or two, although he'd tried hard to hide it. "*Dat* is worried about your brother," she told Eli.

She saw Eli glance at Jacob before returning his attention back to her with a funny look on his face.

Katie took a chilled bottle of root beer out of the refrigerator and handed it to Jacob.

"Where's Hannah?" Annie asked of Katie's youngest child and only daughter.

"She's over at Charlotte's." Katie sat down at the table. "Playing with Ruth Ann."

Jacob lifted his drink with his uninjured hand.

Annie couldn't seem to take her eyes off him as he took a sip and set the glass down on the table. "Jacob—"

He turned and fixed her with a look. "I'm fine, Annie."

Eli raised his eyebrows. "She saw the burn, Jake. Maybe she knows better than you."

"*Ja*, Eli," Annie said. "I think he should see a doctor. He says he is fine, but he's not." She paused. "You said you'd go if your hand appeared worse. Will you go if your *mam* says you should though you may think differently?" she asked him with a quick glance toward his mother.

Jacob sighed. "You'll not rest unless I agree?"

Annie nodded. "If you agree, I won't mention it again."

"Then I agree."

"And I will take a look at it and decide." Katie pushed a plate of lemon squares in Annie's direction.

Annie smiled with satisfaction as she chose one before sliding the plate toward Eli, who sat next to her. Eli took a square and nudged the plate toward Jacob.

Jacob declined the treat and finished his soda. As he

set down the empty bottle, he rose. "If you don't mind, I'm going to head upstairs." He addressed Annie. "*Danki* for dressing my burn and bringing me home."

"Even though you didn't want me to drive?" she challenged.

Jacob's cheeks flushed. "*Ja*, even though." He grabbed the empty soda bottle and set it on the counter near the sink. "Eli, I'll talk with you after you take Annie home."

Eli nodded. "I'll see you later."

Annie finished her tea. "I will talk with you again soon, Jacob," she murmured.

Eli put down his empty cup and stood. "Would you like another?"

"*Nay.* I'm ready to go whenever you are."

Katie rose and gathered the teacups. "Let me help wash those," Annie said as Eli went outside to check on the horse.

"*Nay*, you get home to your *dat*. If I know Joe, he'll be worrying about Jacob." She smiled. "I appreciate the way you took care of him today."

"Jacob is a *gut* man. I'm glad I could help him."

"Jacob may seem too serious at times, but he has a pure heart." Katie tied a work apron about her waist.

"He's been kind to my family, helping me after *Dat's* accident, working in the shop to help my *vadder*." She paused. "He is a *gut* friend."

"Annie?" Eli appeared in the doorway. "Ready?"

She nodded. "The tea and lemon squares were delicious."

Katie smiled. "Say *hallo* to your *mudder* and *vadder*."

Annie nodded and then left, following Eli out of the house and into the buggy. Soon, Eli had steered Janey out onto the main road in the direction of Annie's home.

"You're quiet," Eli said after a time.

"Just thoughtful," she answered.

"He'll be fine, Jacob." He exchanged looks with her. "His hand will heal."

Annie inclined her head. "It shouldn't have happened. He said that no one was at fault, but I wonder…"

Eli raised his eyebrows. "Does it matter?"

She sighed. "*Nay*, I suppose not."

Eli drew up on the leathers as a car passed too swiftly. He frowned. "Careless *Englishers* are going to hurt someone seriously one day."

"*Ja*. Lately, it seems that there are more than the usual tourists in Lancaster County."

"Come to enjoy the fall foliage?" Eli asked.

Annie smiled. "Or to get a *gut* look at us Plain folk."

They chatted easily as Eli drove onto the Zooks' dirt lane and into the barnyard.

"I appreciate the ride, Eli," Annie said with a smile before she climbed out of the buggy.

"I'll see you on Sunday, Annie. *Danki* for taking care of Jacob."

Annie felt her face warm at the mention of Jacob's name. "Will you take him to the doctor if he needs it?"

"*Ja*." Eli tilted his head, then suddenly widened his eyes. "You like him!"

Her heart skipped a beat. "He's my friend."

Eli smiled. "Jacob's a lucky man to have you as his friend."

She felt as if she needed to get away before she said something she shouldn't. "I will see you on Sunday. Will *ya* be going to the youth singing?"

Eli nodded. "*Ja*, I wouldn't miss it." He shifted to face her. "You?"

"I'm thinking about it. I haven't been since before

Dat's accident." Annie leaned in while she talked with Eli. "It should be fun." She started to walk away, then promptly spun back around. "Did *ya* hear that Rebekkah Miller is betrothed? The banns are being posted today."

"She is?" Eli looked thoughtful. "To whom, do you know?"

"Caleb Yoder."

"The new doctor?" he asked, and Annie nodded. "How did you find out?"

She stood back and brushed something off her apron. "I spoke with Reuben the other day."

Eli looked out the front buggy window before turning to give her a twisted smile. "I used to be sweet on her."

"*Ach*, I'm sorry, Eli," Annie said. "I shouldn't have said anything."

He waved it off as if it were of no consequence. "*Nay*, 'tis fine. It was a long time ago. I haven't seen or spoken with Rebekkah in over a year."

Annie inclined her head. "I should get inside. I appreciate the ride." She stepped away from the vehicle. "I'll see you soon." Then she waved and watched as Eli drove away from the house. Images of Jacob intermingled while his brother Eli's words spun in her head.

Jacob Lapp. He was different than his brother but also the same.

She climbed the front stoop and onto the covered porch. Annie froze as emotion hit her with sudden clarity. Why couldn't she stop thinking about Jacob Lapp? Jacob was a *gut* and caring friend, but he was young and handsome, and she didn't want young and handsome. She wanted—needed—calm, peace and an easy affection. She scowled. By suggesting that she consider him, he had made it impossible for her to ignore him.

* * *

Four days after his burn accident, Jacob stood on his front porch, gazing out at the landscape. His hand throbbed, causing him pain. As expected, a huge water blister had risen to cover the injured area. It was only after the blister burst that his mother had suggested that he seek medical help from Jonah Troyer, who gave medical aid to the less serious injuries among the members of their Amish community. Jonah had taken one look at Jacob's hand and frowned.

"You'd best go and see that English doc, Dr. Jamieson," he had told Jacob. "I think you need a prescription. Dr. Jamieson can write you one." And so Jacob had made an appointment with Dr. Jamieson for the next day.

Dr. Jamieson had examined the burn and agreed. "Jonah is right. I'll prescribe an antibiotic cream. Spread it gently over the open burn wound and then keep the burn covered with gauze. Continue to use both until the burn heals."

"When can I go back to work?" Jacob had asked.

Dr. Jamieson had shaken his head. "Stay away from the shop for at least a week. You're going to feel uncomfortable going back too soon. You mustn't do anything to jeopardize the sterile environment of the wound. In other words, Jacob, don't do anything that may cause infection."

Waiting for his family to depart for Sunday church service, Jacob wondered what he was going to do during the coming week. He needed to keep busy. He wasn't allowed to help on the farm, although at this time of year, most of the work was in preparation for next spring's planting. He couldn't work with the animals. He couldn't work in Noah's furniture shop or with Jed for the construction company. Suddenly, the chores he never particularly enjoyed seemed inviting. He wasn't used to being idle, and it didn't sit well with him. In fact, it gave him way too much time to think about Annie and his feelings for her.

Friends, he thought. She said they were friends. If only he were older and had a permanent position…then he'd have a chance with Annie. *Think about me, Annie. Consider me. I can make you happy if only you'll let me.*

Jacob adjusted his Sunday-best black felt hat as he stepped out onto the lawn. He had to decide on his life's path. What were his options? He could work on a farm but not his father's. All monies earned from the Samuel Lapp farm went to provide for his mother and the remaining five siblings, besides him, still living at home.

There was always Noah's furniture shop, but he didn't have his older brother's talent for crafting furniture, and while he could make deliveries for Noah, he couldn't earn a living at it.

He would do anything to show Annie that they were meant to be together. But what if she didn't ever consider him seriously? What if she remained determined to marry a church elder? Someone like Ike King?

His younger brother Daniel burst out of the house and flew down the porch steps. "We're going to be late for Sunday services!"

"I'm ready. I've been ready," Isaac insisted as he joined them.

"We're all ready," his mother said as she exited the house with their youngest brother, Joseph, and Hannah, their little sister.

"Where's *Dat*?" Eli asked as he came up from the yard. He'd brought around the family buggy.

"He's coming," *Mam* said.

"I'm here," their father said as he pulled the front

door shut and locked it. "Let's go." He nodded toward the buggy, parked only a few yards away.

"Aren't you coming, Jacob?" Hannah beamed up at him as she approached and then tugged on his arm.

Jacob smiled at her. Dressed in her Sunday best, she looked adorable. "*Ja*, Hannah. I'm coming."

"Mam?" Isaac said. "What about the food?"

"I took it over to Mae's yesterday."

"Let's go," Samuel urged. "We don't want to be late."

They rode in the buggy because they were running behind, and the vehicle was quicker. If they'd left earlier, they could have easily walked. And Jacob's father had heard that it was going to rain this afternoon.

Samuel drove the short distance down their lane and across the road, onto the Amos King property. Several gray family buggies were already parked in the yard when Jacob's father drove in and halted their vehicle.

Were the Zooks here? Jacob glanced about, longing for a glimpse of Annie. As if the Lord had heard his thoughts, Josiah drove the Zook family into the barn-yard and pulled up directly next to the Lapps' vehicle.

Jacob spied Annie as she exited the buggy, and his spirits rose. She didn't see him as she skirted the vehicle to help her father. Annie pulled out Joe's crutches and set them against the buggy's side before she extended a hand toward her father. Josiah came around to help his sister with Joe. Annie handed the crutches to Joe and then reached into the buggy for the food she'd prepared.

Jacob's family had climbed out of their buggy and headed toward the Amos King farmhouse. With eyes for only Annie, Jacob was slow to follow. Annie turned and caught sight of him.

"Jacob." She smiled at him, and heart pumping hard,

he waited for her. "How is your hand?" she asked. She sounded breathless.

"Let me carry this for you." He reached for her plate before she had a chance to refuse, and he held it against him with his good hand. They fell into step together as they approached the house. "My hand is healing well." He flashed her glance. "Because of you." He smiled as he caressed her with his gaze. "How is Joe?"

She blinked as if taken aback. "*Dat's* fine." Annie looked pretty in her Sunday-best dark green dress with white cape and apron. Her white head covering, or prayer *kapp*, revealed a glimpse of her golden-blond hair.

"No more buggy rides with any older men?" he asked, watching her carefully.

"*Nay* and no new, prospective husband candidates. Thanks be to God."

"Did you think about what I said?" He watched her carefully.

She grew still. "Said?"

He nodded. "About me."

"Jacob—"

"Jake!" Eli interrupted from inside the house. "Are you coming?"

"*Ja*, in a minute! I'm helping Annie." As they reached the steps, Jacob gestured for Annie to precede him. He saw that she was blushing. He handed her the covered dish. "Annie—" He stopped, looked at her. She looked awkward, dismayed. Now wasn't the time to talk seriously with her. "What did you make?" he asked with a smile. "Whatever is in there smells wonderful."

"You'll have to wait until after Sunday service to find out," she replied. He watched her visibly relax.

"But I carried it all the way up here for you." He pretended to be sad.

"And *ya* handled the weight well," she quipped.

Jacob laughed outright. He couldn't help it; Annie looked so cute with that determined expression on her face and the teasing twinkle in her blue eyes. He felt hopeful. He quieted his laugh to a soft chuckle. Folks were gathering inside the house for church service. He didn't want to draw unwanted attention to himself or Annie.

"I hope that whatever you made is worth waiting for," he said.

"Worth is entirely your opinion and of no consequence to me," she replied crisply. She turned abruptly and marched across the lawn toward the kitchen area of the house.

Amused by her attitude, Jacob watched her stalk off. He grinned.

Anger was better than indifference.

Chapter Twelve

Seated between her mother and sister, Annie listened as Levi Stoltzfus gave the Sunday sermon. He was a good speaker, reminding all about the importance of God in life and about family values. He spoke of the *Ordnung*, the teachings of the Amish faith, and he spoke of it with eloquence.

She became aware of Charlotte King Peachy, Abram's wife, who sat with Abram's five children. Charlotte glanced frequently and with affection toward her husband across the room. He beamed back at her while he attempted to keep focused on Preacher Levi's words.

She wanted a relationship like theirs, Annie thought. A man to love and marry and be a good father to their children.

She sensed someone's regard and turned to discover Ike. The man smiled. Ike was a nice man as well as a good member of the Happiness community. He was also Amos King's younger brother.

She felt the impact of someone else's stare and locked gazes with Jacob Lapp, seated on the bench behind Ike. His tawny gaze was sharp, and he didn't smile. He con-

tinued to gawk at her without expression before returning his attention to the preacher's sermon.

Annie felt her cheeks burning. Pulse thrumming, she
forced her attention back to Ike King. Ike was looking for
a wife and he wanted a family. Ike was older, safe. She
could marry someone like Ike and be happy.

Couldn't she?

She couldn't consider Jacob. It wouldn't be wise. Yet,
she couldn't ignore that she had feelings for the man.

Annie straightened in her seat, unwavering in her decision to put a plan in motion that would keep her on her
determined path. She would talk with Ike, see if he was
interested in walking out with her.

Why would Jacob want a woman who was two years
older and afraid of getting hurt?

She felt her mother's regard, saw her displeasure,
and straightened as she focused on the sermon again.
She joined in loudly as the congregation sang a hymn.
Their chanting voices blended beautifully, and Annie got
caught up in the song. She pushed all of her concerns
away as she prayed to the Lord and asked His help. A
sense of peace overcame her; the Lord's way of showing
her His presence. And she smiled. Everything would be
fine. God would guide her in the right direction. All she
had to do was pray hard and believe.

Church service ended, and Jacob stood on the front
porch leaning against the railing. Seeing Annie again
was like a kick to his midsection. He had put his heart
on the line for her, throwing out the idea that they could
be sweethearts rather than friends. If she had given it
any serious thought, Annie gave no sign.

I should have listened to Eli. His brother had warned
him to stay away from the Zook family farm.

There was a singing tonight. Should he go? Annie probably wouldn't attend, not if she planned to marry Ike King. He'd go, have fun and flirt a little with one of the other girls.

He frowned. *As if I could.* He loved Annie too much to even think of spending time with another woman.

At some point he would return to work at the blacksmithy. But he would keep his distance from Annie. If she was interested in a relationship with him, then she would have to make the next move.

"What are you doing out here?" Eli stepped up to lean against the porch railing next to Jacob.

"Just thinking about tonight's singing…"

Eli scowled. "You are planning to go?" He leaned closer to whisper in Jacob's ear. "Or are you going to let Annie Zook stop you from enjoying yourself?" He ran a hand through his blond hair. Like the rest of the men, he removed his hat before attending church. "You need to show Annie that you are fine without her."

"I already decided to go."

Eli's mouth opened and closed. *"Gut,"* he said finally.

Jacob chuckled. "Almost speechless. That's new for you."

"Jacob! Eli!" Amos and Mae King's son John, affectionately called BJ or Big John after Amos's eldest daughter, Sarah, and her husband, Eli, had chosen little John for their baby son. "My *vadder* has been looking for you," BJ said. "He wants to know if you'll help with the church. He wants to move several benches into the other room."

Jacob pushed off the railing, and Eli followed. "Any *gut* food waiting inside for us?" he asked the boy.

"Lots of *gut* food. I've got a hankering for a big helping of apple crisp."

Eli smiled as he grabbed hold of the screen door and held it open as they stepped inside. "I've a yearning for a slice of spice cake or a helping of chocolate cream pudding."

With Eli's help, Jacob moved benches into the other room. His thoughts turned to Annie. *I wonder what she made today.* Whatever it was—cake, pie or sheet cookie, it would taste delicious.

Eli's voice interrupted his train of thought. "Let's grab these and take them outside."

Jacob worked with his brother and the two King boys until all the benches were either set up inside or outside in the yard, for those wishing to enjoy the warm autumn day.

By the time he and Eli were done, Jacob felt in control of his emotions again. He would go to the singing and would have a good time…without Annie Zook.

Annie rode to the singing with her two brothers. Josiah climbed out of the buggy and headed straight for Nancy King, who stood outside waiting for him. Peter lingered as Annie reached into the back of the vehicle to pick up the nearest of two snack platters she'd prepared for the evening.

Her brother was studying the people who chatted outside the barn. This was Peter's first singing and he had been eager to come. She smiled. "Are you ready?"

Peter rewarded her with a grin. *"Ja."* A buggy arrived bringing more friends. "There's Reuben Miller," he said as he lifted a hand to wave.

"I see him." Annie suddenly remembered Reuben's offer to take her home. She was startled to realize that she hadn't given the young man any thought since their last encounter over a week and a half ago. Except when she'd spoken of him to Jacob.

"I don't see Rebekkah," Peter noticed.

"You won't," Annie said. "She's betrothed." She handed him the platter.

"*Ach, ja*, I'd forgotten." He accepted the plate of lemon squares. "What about the gingerbread cake?"

"I'll get it." Annie reached to retrieve the gingerbread cake with cream-cheese frosting.

Another buggy pulled in to park on the other side. The Lapp twin brothers stepped out, and Annie watched their approach with her heart thundering in startling awareness of Jacob.

"*Hallo*, Annie," Eli greeted. "Peter, I'm glad to see you here."

Annie locked eyes with Jacob. "Jacob," she said.

Jacob gave her a solemn nod. "Annie."

Eli and Peter chatted as they headed toward the barn. Annie had no choice but to follow, with Jacob accompanying her. She couldn't help but notice how handsome he was. He cut a fine figure in his Sunday best. His black vest and white shirt fit him well as did his black pants with black shoes. The brim of his black felt hat shielded his eyes, but Annie could tell when he was looking at her. It was evening, and the setting sun was beautiful, a fiery orb that had changed the sky to colorful splashes of bright orange interwoven with red. The evening was quiet, and Annie felt the tension between them vibrate in the night air.

"Your hand looks better," she said after desperately searching for something to say.

"*Ja*, 'tis much improved," he said, sounding amused. Jacob had nothing to add to keep up the flow of conversation.

"I need to go," Annie began.

"Annie." The intensity in Jacob's voice stopped her. *"Ja?"*

"We need to talk later. We haven't talked in ages."

Annie nodded. Leaving Jacob's side after they entered the barn together, Annie placed the gingerbread cake with the rest of the snack food.

A long table with chairs had been set up in the barn. Girls were seated on one side and boys on the other. Annie took the first available seat, and to her dismay, Joseph Byler appeared and sat down across from her.

"Hello, Annie," he said with a sloppy smile.

Annie nodded. His presence dampened her enjoyment of the evening. "Joseph."

"Annie!" Reuben Miller stepped into the room and took a seat next to Joseph. "I told *ya* I would come."

She smiled; she couldn't help it. "I take it the banns were posted for Rebekkah and Caleb."

Reuben nodded. *"Ja,* and everyone is happy about the union."

Jacob sat on Joseph's other side. "Joseph," he greeted. He eyed Reuben over Joseph's head. "How are *ya,* Reuben?" He took off his hat and set it on the table, rewarding Annie with a good view of his features. His brown hair shone in the gas-lantern light, and there was a tiny smile playing about his masculine lips.

Her heart beat a rapid tattoo as she compared him to the two other men. Jacob Lapp was easily the most handsome.

Her brother Josiah opened his copy of the *Ausbund* and led them in the first song. He flashed Nancy a smile before he began to sing his chosen hymn in a deep, confident voice. Eli Lapp joined in, followed by the other young people. Annie couldn't keep her eyes off Jacob as he raised his voice in song, his tone strong, melodic and pleasant.

Caught up in the moment, Annie sang out for God and for the sure joy of it. Jacob captured her attention and Annie was surprised to see his golden eyes fill with warmth as they held gazes and joined voices.

A while later, at Nancy's urging, Josiah called a refreshment break. Anne rose along with the other girls to unwrap the food, while the young men stood to chat and stretch their legs. Nancy had made lemonade, and someone had brought homemade birch beer. Mae King, Nancy's mother, had provided hot tea and coffee as the days were cool and the nights could be downright cold. Soon everyone enjoyed paper plates filled with goodies and the beverage of their choice.

Annie was nursing a cup of hot tea, when Joseph Byler approached.

"Annie," he said, "did you make these brownies?"

Annie shook her head. "Meg Stoltzfus did."

He turned with a frown to eye the snack table, and as he did, Reuben Miller slid into his place in front of Annie.

"Annie," he greeted with a smile. "This is yours. I can tell." He referred to her gingerbread cake.

"How?" Annie asked. She wondered how he'd known.

He grinned. "Because it's the most delicious item on the table." He lowered his voice. "And Peter told me."

Annie laughed.

"May I take *ya* home this evening?" he asked, fulfilling her worst fears.

"I—"

"I'm afraid to disappoint you, but she's riding with me this evening," Jacob said as he joined them.

Annie's heart began to race as soon as she heard Jacob's voice.

Reuben glanced from Jacob to Annie, who didn't refute Jacob's claim. "I see."

"I appreciate the offer, Reuben," Annie said while shooting Jacob a look, "but yes, Jacob will be taking me home."

Joseph Byler, who'd been shifted outside the circle, returned with another snack on his plate. "This one must be yours," he told Annie.

Jacob didn't move, and Annie was stunned by his desire to linger.

Sensing Joseph's confusion, she glanced at his plate. "*Ja*, I made that one."

Joseph glanced toward Jacob and frowned as Jacob shifted closer to Annie's side. The young man widened his eyes and scurried away.

"So, you'll be taking me home, will you?" she said softly.

"You wanted to be rescued, didn't *ya*?" He took a bite of a lemon square. "These are delicious, Annie," he said, sounding sincere. "You are an excellent cook and baker." He lowered his voice conspiratorially. "And your *mudder* didn't have to point it out to me. I just knew."

Annie laughed, and the earlier awkwardness between them suddenly vanished. "I'm glad you like them." Reuben had already moved on to talk to Meg Stoltzfus. Joseph, on the other hand, continued to watch her from a distance, with a pouting look on his face.

Jacob followed the direction of her gaze. "He's not happy."

"*Nay.*" She gave Jacob a crooked smile. "He doesn't take a hint well."

"I can't speak for Joseph. He is a determined man,

but I think he is harmless. Eventually he'll get the hint. You mustn't worry too much about him."

"And how many times will you have to rescue me from him before he'll understand that I'm just not interested in him?"

"If I'm not available, you can ask someone else to rescue you, like Eli or Ike King," he said softly.

Annie felt keen disappointment. "I'm sorry. I didn't mean to impose."

Jacob narrowed his eyes. "I offered to take you home and you accepted. How is that an imposition?"

"It's not?" She waited with a wildly beating heart for his answer.

"*Nay*, taking you home can never be an imposition," he said, and Annie felt joy at his words. "After all, we're friends, aren't we?" He shot a look over his shoulder. "'Tis time to go back inside."

She nodded and set down her teacup. *Friends*, she thought. He *had* been teasing her when he'd suggested a possible deeper relationship between them. When she headed back inside, she was surprised to find that Jacob had waited for her.

She resumed her seat in the other room and was startled when Jacob took the chair directly across from her. Joseph frowned and shifted to the seat that Jacob had vacated earlier. Jacob smiled at her, and Annie knew a warmth and pleasure she'd never felt with his older brother Jed. When Jacob raised an eyebrow at her, she felt her heart soar. She wondered what it would be like to hold hands with him, then scolded herself for foolishly entertaining the thought. She blushed when she saw Jacob eyeing her with curiosity.

The singing resumed with Peter's choice of hymn. As her brother began to sing, Annie watched Jacob, loving the way he'd made her feel, recalling all the wonderful things he'd done for her and her family. She had a sudden mental image of living with him as man and wife. *What am I doing?* Setting herself up for heartbreak, she thought.

The evening passed quickly, and soon everyone rose to leave. A few of the young men and women coupled up and walked out into the night together. Annie headed out the door alone, disappointed that Jacob had gone outside without her. Still, she was grateful for the reprieve. She was confused, wanting one thing but afraid of what could happen if she gave in.

The night was chilly, and Annie hugged herself with her arms as she waited and wondered if Jacob had forgotten her.

Josiah approached. "Annie, I'm going to stay awhile with Nancy," he said. "Will *ya* be able to get a ride home?"

She smiled. "I have a ride." Josiah looked surprised but pleased, yet his curiosity about whom she was referring to wasn't stronger than his desire to return to Nancy.

"Are you ready?" Jacob appeared out of nowhere, startling her, causing her heart to jump.

She nodded. Following him, Annie anticipated the ride home with excitement. She knew it was wrong to put her heart at risk, but she couldn't help it. It was one night; surely, she could enjoy one night in Jacob Lapp's company and still keep her heart intact.

Chapter Thirteen

Jacob gestured for Annie to precede him as they headed toward his family's market wagon. His brother Eli and Mary Hershberger, Annie's cousin, were already in the open wagon bed along with Annie's youngest brother, Peter.

He felt Annie hesitate before continuing, almost as if she was startled to learn that others would be riding home with them. He recalled the way Annie had laughed and spoken with Ike King earlier in the day and decided that he was mistaken, especially after she'd greeted the occupants of the wagon cheerfully.

He followed her to the passenger side of the vehicle's front bench seat and extended his hand to assist her up. She looked at him for a heartbeat, before she placed her fingers within his grasp. As he helped her onto the bench, Jacob was not unaffected by the warmth of her small hand within his. He drew a sharp breath as he released his grip and hurried to the other side, where he climbed in. Emotion slammed in his chest. He wanted to take her in his arms and whirl her away to a place where they could be alone. He was conscious of Annie beside him as he picked up the reins and spurred the horse on.

He heard conversation and laughter from the back of the wagon. Annie's brother Peter needed a ride, and Eli had offered to take him home. They arrived at the Hershberger farm first, and Jacob pulled into the barnyard and waited as Eli walked Mary Hershberger to her door. He wondered what Annie was thinking as she watched Eli and Mary before turning to stare straight ahead.

"You look lovely tonight," he said softly. There was enough moonlight for him to see her. The sight of her stole his breath away.

Annie shot him a glance in the darkness. She was quiet a moment. "You're just being kind."

"I wasn't being kind, Annie," he admitted. His fingers reached for hers. She jumped at his touch, as if startled, and he quickly withdrew his hand.

"Jacob?" she whispered.

He turned, stared at her, saw the look in her eyes and was tempted to reach for her hand again. But he didn't, for he saw indecision and dismay in her expression. He shrugged and smiled at her instead. "It's all right, Annie." He heard her sigh and wondered what she was thinking.

Soon, his brother had returned. Eli hopped into the back of the wagon, and Jacob steered the horse back to the main road and on toward the Joseph Zook farm.

"How did you like your first singing, Pete?" Eli asked.

"It was fun." Jacob couldn't see Peter's face, but he could imagine the boy's delight. "I like Meg Hostetler," he confessed.

"She's our cousin," Eli said.

"She's a nice girl," Peter replied.

"*Ja*, and don't *ya* forget it," Eli warned, but Jacob could hear laughter in his brother's voice.

Peter was silent for a moment, as if taking Eli's warning seriously. "I won't."

Reaching the road to the Zook farmhouse, Jacob
turned on the battery-operated turn signal and steered
the horse left onto the dirt lane. He wanted to kiss her,
he thought. If only they were alone…

He reined in the horse in the barnyard and sat still for
several seconds. Then he jumped down from the vehicle,
walked around the wagon to Annie's side and offered his
hand to her. As he waited a heartbeat, Jacob remembered
another time when he'd offered her his hand and she'd
chosen to ignore his help. This time, to his delight, she
accepted it, and he enjoyed the feeling of holding her
hand. There was warmth where they touched. Jacob experienced tightness in his chest when Annie gave him a
tremulous smile. He released her fingers as her brother
scrambled out of the back of the wagon.

"I appreciate the ride," Peter said before he hurried
inside the house and shut the door.

Eli climbed from the back of the wagon onto the front
seat as Jacob accompanied Annie to her door.

"I didn't get a chance to tell you," Jacob said huskily,
"but I wanted to be alone with you tonight."

He felt her surprise and wondered if he should have
kept his mouth shut. But then she smiled and her blue
eyes shone in the moonlight and the golden glow from
the lamplight glimmering from inside the house, through
the windows.

"You did?" He saw her glance toward the wagon and
Eli, who waited patiently up front.

He nodded, reached for her hand again. He rubbed his
thumb over her soft skin. "We need to talk—"

"Jacob—"

He leaned in and kissed her, catching her off guard.

"Jacob…"

"Annie?" Her sister Barbara stood just inside the doorway.

Annie stepped back, out of reach, and Jacob wondered if Barbara had witnessed their kiss. "I'll be inside in a minute."

He inwardly scolded himself for wanting to spend more time with her. "I should say *gut* night, Annie."

"Jacob," she whispered. She stared at him a moment and then leaned forward.

Jacob saw the longing in her blue gaze and started to reach for her.

"Annie," Barbara called.

"I have to go." Her eyes sparkled in the lantern light. "*Gut* night, Jacob," she murmured. Then she disappeared into the house, without looking back.

Jacob returned to the wagon, where his brother waited with a knowing look.

"You love her," Eli accused.

Jacob sighed. "We're just friends."

"But you want to be more."

He shrugged as he pulled the brim of his hat down low. "I'll get over it." His heart thumped hard as he recalled the sweet taste of her lips and the way she'd hovered as if she wanted him to kiss her again.

Eli shook his head as he picked up the leathers. "I think not, brother," he said, and he drove the horse toward home.

"What's between you and Mary Hershberger?" Jacob asked Eli.

"Nothing. We were just having a *gut* time. Mary has her heart set on someone else."

Jacob made a noise of disbelief. "And she told you this?"

Eli grinned at him. "*Nay*, but I can tell. Didn't ya see how she was watching Joseph this evening?"

"Joseph Byler?" Jacob was surprised.

"*Ja.*"

He laughed. Jacob couldn't help himself. Joseph liked Annie, but Mary Hershberger liked Joseph, while he liked Annie, who liked…Ike King. *Or maybe not.* There had been a flash of something in her blue eyes, her response to his quick kiss, before she'd gone into the house, that made him wonder.

"And you?" Jacob asked. "Have you got your heart set on anyone in particular?"

Eli shook his head. "I'm in no hurry to find a sweetheart. 'Tis more fun to watch the drama of you and Annie."

He didn't think Eli had seen their kiss. It had been dark, and Jacob had made it a quick one. "There is no drama between Annie and me."

Eli looked unconvinced. "If you say so, *bruder*."

Inside the house, through the window, Annie watched Jacob and Eli drive off in the wagon. Her lips still tingled from his surprising kiss. *Why did he kiss me?* After a kiss like that, how was she to remember all the reasons why she'd wanted to avoid him?

Jacob had stepped in this evening to prevent Reuben or Joseph from taking her home. It was as if he'd read her mind and suddenly he'd been there to rescue her. She knew he had helped out of friendship. Though that kiss was more than friendly…

Annie left the window and went upstairs to her room. Barbara had gone up to bed, and she was eager to speak with her. Levi Stoltzfus had come to dinner again, and Barbara had chosen to stay home to spend time with him.

"How did things go?" Annie asked Barbara as she started to undress.

Barbara was quiet. "You're not mad that I'm seeing him?"

Annie stopped and stared. "Why should I be? I can tell that he cares for you."

"You can?" Barbara sounded pleased.

"*Ja*, he is a *gut* man, and I think you and he will do well together."

"I'm glad you feel that way." Barbara moved to sit up against the headboard. "Levi and I went for a walk after dinner."

Annie widened her eyes. "You did?" She took off her prayer *kapp* and unpinned her long hair.

A soft smile played about his lips. "*Ja*, and *Mam* didn't mind. She and *Dat* said I could go with him." Barbara sighed dreamily. "We went through the yard and then across the fields. The moon was bright, and I could see his face." Barbara ran fingers through her long dark unbound hair. "He is so handsome. And he seemed to enjoy himself." She sighed. "I loved every minute with him."

"You love him." Annie smiled as she pulled back the quilt and climbed into bed beside her sister.

She sensed Barbara's surprise, but her voice was soft as she said, *"Ja."*

"That's *gut*!" Annie assured her.

"You must think me foolish," Barbara said. "I fell for David, and now it's only been a little over a month, and I've fallen in love with Levi Stoltzfus." She paused. "But this feels different."

"I don't think you foolish at all," Annie assured her. "You have known Levi your entire life. You know who he is and the type of man he's become." She climbed into bed next to Barbara. "David Byler was just an infatuation. By your own admission, he was a *gut*-looking boy, and you were flattered by his attention. He lives in New Wilmington while you belong here. Levi is here—why shouldn't you allow yourself to love him?"

"I can't be sure he loves me," Barbara said, "or if he is just being nice."

"Enjoy your time with him, and you'll know. Whatever happens, I want you to be happy."

"Even if Levi Stoltzfus is no long available?"

Annie chuckled as she slid down under the bed quilt and stared at the ceiling. "I want to marry an older man. But did I say it has to be Levi?" She met Barbara's gaze. "*Nay*, it was *Mam's* idea to encourage him in my direction."

"I could be happy spending my whole life with him," Barbara said. She blew out the candle, then settled in next to Annie. "I hope you find someone soon."

Annie sighed. "What will be, will be. I can't know God's will until He shows it to me. I'll be fine. You worry about yourself and stop fretting over my future."

"I love you, Annie," Barbara whispered into the dark.

"I love you, Barbara. *Gut* night." While she drifted off to sleep, Annie thought of Jacob, knowing that she shouldn't be giving advice to others when she couldn't make up her mind about her own future.

"Are you heading to the Zooks'?" Eli asked as he worked alongside Jacob in the barn.

"*Nay*. Maybe later this afternoon." His hand was bothering him. Although it was healing, he still kept it covered. The large blister formed by the second-degree burn had popped, and the skin was still tender, but the wound itself looked much better.

"What about Joe?" his brother asked as he mucked out the stable.

Jacob filled a feed pail for Janey and set it within her reach. He checked to make sure she had water and then moved on to the other horses.

"Joe knows I'll be back eventually. He's the one who wanted to make sure my hand was healed properly before starting back to work."

"But it's not your hand that's keeping you away now," Eli said with the keen sense of knowing his brother well. "It's Annie."

"She can't keep me from helping Joe." Jacob finished with the horses and moved to feed *Mam's* chickens. His brother had it right. It was Annie who made him reluctant to return. He had kissed her, and now he was afraid that in the end, he'd be left alone as she chose to wed Ike King.

Finished with one stall, Eli moved on to the next one. "Why don't you just tell her how you feel?"

Jacob watched his brother's progress. "You missed something," he said with amusement.

"You're enjoying this, aren't you?" Eli glared with feigned anger at his brother, who was older by four minutes. "You get the easy chores while I handle this—" He gestured toward the wheelbarrow that held horse manure.

"I can't risk getting my hand dirty."

"You're avoiding an answer," Eli said.

"Annie Zook has her heart set on marrying someone like Ike King. The woman can't seem to make up her mind," Jacob said.

"But she doesn't know how long you've had feelings for her. What if she likes you more than she's let on?" Eli said. Finished with the stalls, he lifted the handles of the wheelbarrow and pushed it outside. Jacob followed behind, a bucket of chicken feed in his uninjured hand.

Jacob dipped his fingers into the grain and tossed it onto the ground, among the fowl. The birds clucked and moved about excitedly before they pecked at their meal.

Annie had been too surprised to kiss him back last night, but he feared he was mistaken in that she wanted to. "She does like me," Jacob admitted, "as a friend."

"A *gut* friend." Eli swatted a fly on his neck.

"*Ja*, perhaps." Jacob threw feed in another direction and the chickens found their way to the newly tossed grain. "But sometimes being a friend isn't enough."

Eli sighed. "So you hope your feelings will go away."

Jacob had gone back and forth in his mind about whether or not he should continue to pursue Annie. He wanted to be with her. But he had no idea if she'd changed her plans. What if she still wanted to marry an older man?

"Why not go after her? What if she's changed her mind and wants someone like you?" Eli went to dump the refuse in a designated area.

Should he try? Should he confront her, tell her of his feelings, risk all in the hope that she might return his love?

Eli returned with the empty wheelbarrow. "Are you going to Joe's this afternoon or not?"

"I don't know." Something inside urged him to go, while another side of him caused him to hesitate. "I'm still deciding."

"Think about going. If you see Annie, talk with her. If you don't, you'll regret that you missed an opportunity to win her love."

After Eli left, Jacob put away the empty chicken-feed bucket and headed toward the house. He could go to the blacksmith shop to work. He wouldn't let Joe down, no matter how difficult circumstances might become for him. *Annie*, he thought. He wanted to see her, talk with her…and reach across a bench seat in the dark to capture her hand.

Chapter Fourteen

"*Mam!* I'm going to take Jacob breakfast!" Annie called as she headed toward the door with a thermos and a covered plate of food.

"That's fine, Annie," *Mam* said as she came out of the gathering room with corn broom in hand. "Don't be long. We've got a lot to do today."

"I won't be," she promised. Annie found she was eager to see Jacob. Had she imagined the attraction between them? Or had she simply dreamed of their kiss? She hurried across the yard, the jug in one hand, a plate of sticky buns in the other and a smile on her face. When she reached the shop, she experienced a tremor of excitement.

"Jacob?" she called as she opened the door to the building.

The shop was quiet, too quiet. Annie frowned. There was no light inside the building, no ring of steel against iron.

"Jacob?" she said hesitantly. She moved to stand in the inner doorway and stared inside. Everything was as neat as a pin, just as Peter and *Dat* had left it after Jacob's accident.

Where was Jacob? He had been well enough to attend the singing. And he'd offered his hand to help her onto the wagon. She became concerned. Had he done too much yesterday? Had he reinjured his hand?

Where is he? She longed to see him in his leather apron, heating metal until it glowed red, raising the tongs to inspect the fiery red piece before setting it on the anvil to hammer into shape. She recalled how he looked, his eyes narrowed as he concentrated on the task, the movement of his forearms as he brought down the hammer again and again, fired up the metal and repeated the process. She felt an odd feeling in her chest at the mental image.

Annie left the thermos on the worktable in case Jacob came later. She eyed the plate of sticky buns and decided it would be fine to leave them, too. As she left the shop and headed back toward the house, she felt a rush of disappointment. *Mam* said that they had much to do today. It was just as well that Jacob wasn't here, for she had no time to visit with him this morning.

What if he regretted kissing her? she thought. What if he'd simply tried to prove a point? All the more reason for her to avoid him.

Annie walked slowly back to the house, wondering why it felt as if the sunshine and joy had been stolen from her day. She had to stop thinking the worst. She would see and talk with Jacob another day. She'd have to be satisfied with that. She picked up her pace and ran toward the porch steps. "*Mam!* I'm back! What would you like me to do first?"

There was no one around when Jacob arrived at Horseshoe Joe's. His brother had needed to run errands in town, so Eli had brought him with the promise to return for him later.

There was no sign of anyone in the yard, no sign of movement in the farmhouse windows. He entered the shop and pushed open a window to allow the sunlight inside. Then, he checked the work ledger to see what needed to be done. William Mast—handsaw repair. Bob Whittier—metal coat hooks.

He continued down the list. Arlin Stoltzfus requested that he make some shepherd's hooks, like *Englishers* liked to use in their front yards, on which to hang flower pots or wind chimes. The cold weather was an impending threat, and several neighbors had appointments for him to replace their horses' and mules' shoes.

He glanced toward the vise mounted on one end of the worktable. As he took down his leather apron, he caught sight of a thermos and a plate of sticky buns. *Annie.* He smiled. He wasn't ready to see her yet, but it was comforting to know that she cared enough to bring him breakfast. Laying the apron across the top of the worktable, he paused to pour himself a cup of coffee. After a few slow sips, he sighed appreciatively. The woman always remembered how he liked it best. The plate of sticky buns tempted him, making his mouth water, for he had eaten breakfast hours ago before helping his brothers around the farm. One delicious bite of the bun led to another until he had finished the first and started on a second one. Wouldn't it be wonderful if he had her in his life always! Then he scolded himself for being distracted by her.

Forcing her from his mind, Jacob focused on the work. He donned his apron and pulled on gloves to protect his hands. As canvas and leather brushed his burn injury, he winced, but then the pain passed and he was ready to begin. He grabbed solid iron pieces from a shelf and set them on the worktable. Then he reached for a pair of recently purchased safety glasses and put them on. He readied the forge, grabbed his metal tongs and cross-peen hammer and went to work.

"Annie!" *Mam's* voice came from the bottom of the stairs.

"Ja?" Annie left her brothers' bedroom to look down at her from the top landing. "Do you need me?"

"I'd like you and your sister to run an errand for me."

"I'll be right down." Annie returned to the bedroom and grabbed the sheets she'd stripped off the two beds.

Mam and Barbara were in the kitchen when Annie came downstairs. *Mam* stood near the stove, ladling homemade soup into a large bowl. When she was done, she turned to her daughters. "I'd like you to take this chicken soup over to Ike King."

Annie exchanged glances with her sister. "Is he ill?" she asked.

Mam nodded. "Josie stopped by on her way to Whittier's Store. She said he has stomach pains." She worked as she talked, withdrawing a sleeve of saltines from the pantry and setting them near the soup bowl.

"Do you think we should bring him chamomile tea?" Barbara suggested. "He may want a cup to settle his stomach."

"That's a fine idea, Barbara," *Mam* said.

Annie pitched in to gather things to take to Ike. Her mother's concern for him alleviated the fear that this was a way for *Mam* to get her into Ike's company. She didn't think her mother was trying to make her a match—this time.

When she was done preparing Ike's care package, *Mam* gave Barbara a plastic bag with the crackers, one of her home remedies for stomachaches and the chamomile tea.

"Annie, you take the soup," *Mam* instructed. "Barbara, put some paper bowls in the bag so there will be no dirty dishes to wash."

Soon, the sisters were in the buggy, with Annie steering the horse toward Ike King's farm. They arrived within minutes. Annie parked their vehicle in Ike's barnyard, and the sisters climbed out.

"Shall we knock or just call out?" Barbara asked as they approached the house.

"Why not do both?" Annie shifted the bowl of soup to one arm as she climbed the porch steps. She tapped lightly on the wooden door. "It's a big place," she commented. Ike's home was an impressive two-story whitewashed brick farmhouse.

Annie rapped on the door again. "Ike?" When there was no response, she grew concerned. She knocked harder. *"Ike?"*

"What do we do if he doesn't answer?" Barbara peered inside a window. "I don't see him."

Annie thought a moment. "If he doesn't come, we'll go around to the back. He might have fallen asleep in a chair."

"Let's try again," Barbara suggested. This time she knocked. *"Ike!"*

Finally, they heard movement inside and then the door opened. Ike stood on the threshold, looking ill and with his hair mussed up as if he'd run his fingers through it. He appeared disoriented at first, and his eyes widened as realization dawned. "Annie!" he said. "Barbara."

"We heard you were feeling poorly," Annie explained with a sympathetic smile. "We've brought soup and crackers and some chamomile tea to settle your stomach. *Mam* sent some of her bellyache medicine."

"Danki." He moved aside to allow them to enter. Suddenly, he gasped, "I'm sorry, I have to—" And he ran out of the room.

Annie set the soup on his kitchen counter while Barbara took items out of the paper bag.

Minutes later, Ike returned, looking green in the face. His eyes had a glassy look to them as he stood teetering on unsteady legs.

"Sit down, Ike," Anne urged. "Would you like some chicken soup?" She held up *Mam's* bowl.

Ike agreed, and Annie went to work heating it. After Ike ate and returned to rest on the sofa in his gathering room, Annie and Barbara left. Once home, Annie went inside the farmhouse while Barbara headed toward the clothesline to check on the garments they'd hung earlier.

Peter was at the kitchen table when Annie walked in. "Where have you been?" he asked as he munched on a cookie.

"Ike King's. He's ill, and *Mam* wanted him to have some of her chicken soup.

Her brother set his glass down after taking a drink of milk. "He didn't look sick yesterday," he said as he reached for another cookie.

"He's sick today. He looks awful." Annie grabbed Peter's now empty glass and held it up. "More?"

He nodded. She picked up the jug from the counter when she spied the thermos sitting in the dish drainer. "Did you bring this in from *Dat's* shop?" she asked.

"Nay. Jacob brought it before he left earlier. He said the coffee—and the sticky buns—were *gut."*

"Jacob was here?" Recalling his kiss, Annie felt a short burst of joy but then was disappointed when she realized that he'd left and she missed him. "Is he coming tomorrow?" she asked casually as she handed her brother his milk.

Peter shrugged as he drank from his glass. "He didn't say."

Annie stared out the kitchen window. He'd kissed her. It could mean nothing. Handsome young men were always trying to catch women off guard.

She frowned. Kiss or not, handsome young men like Jacob were not in her plans, while someone like Ike would be the husband she needed. But was Ike really what she wanted? Or did she want Jacob?

She recalled Jacob's golden gaze, his warm smile, the feelings she had whenever he was near. Annie hugged herself with her arms. She had done the unthinkable. She had fallen in love with Jacob Lapp, and there was nothing she could do to stop it. *Except to walk away, keep to the plan and marry someone like Ike.*

Two days later...

"Annie." Ike stood a few feet away from the clothesline where Annie worked hanging laundry.

"Ike!" Surprised to see him, she faced him with a smile. "You're looking well."

"I'm feeling better." Ike was an attractive man in his late thirties with sandy-brown hair and a matching beard that edged along the line of his chin. His pale blue eyes twinkled with good health. "It was *gut* of you to bring me soup."

"*Mam* made it." She secured her brother's shirt on the rope with clothespins. "Have you brought work for Jacob?"

"*Nay*, I've brought back your *mudder's* dish. The chicken soup was delicious. It made me feel better."

"I'm glad to hear it." She faced him, squinted against the sun, then held her hand up to shield her eyes. "*Mam* is a wonderful cook."

"So are you," he said with a small smile. "I've tasted your cakes and pies."

Annie felt her face turn warm. "My sister can cook, as well."

He glanced toward the house. "Where is Barbara?" he asked, and Annie was relieved at the switch in the topic of conversation.

"Inside. Why don't you go in for a visit? My *mudder* will make you tea and give you some fresh-baked cookies."

Ike appraised her with an intensity that gave her pause. "And you?" His voice was soft. "Will you be coming up to the *haus*?"

"*Ja*, as soon as I finish here."

"Then I will see you when you are done." Ike smiled at her and then headed toward the farmhouse.

Annie went back to hanging clothes. When she was done, she picked up the laundry basket and strode toward the house. She stopped suddenly and changed directions, moving toward her father's blacksmith shop, her thoughts now focused on Jacob Lapp.

She hadn't seen him this morning. In fact, she hadn't seen them since he'd kissed her the night of the singing. He was avoiding her. Why?

Because he regretted the kiss and their time together? She needed to know.

Again Annie halted and turned back to the house. Why was she chasing Jacob, a man who clearly bemoaned his time with her, when there was Ike—a *gut*, hardworking, caring man—waiting in the house for her?

She retraced her steps until she reached the back porch. As she pushed the door inward, she could hear Ike and *Mam* talking. Ike's voice was easily recognizable from the kitchen.

Annie sighed. The sound of his voice might not incite butterflies in her stomach or make her breath catch, like Jacob's did, but it was kind and gentle and she was drawn to the sound. She set the basket near the bottom of the stairs and went to the kitchen. *"Hallo,"* she greeted with a smile. Ike, Barbara, *Mam* and *Dat* were seated at the table, each with a steaming cup of tea in front of them.

She crossed the room to take out a cup for herself. "What's that delicious aroma?" she asked.

"Cinnamon rolls," *Mam* said. "I'm warming the buns you made this morning."

"They smell wonderful." Ike flashed Annie an appreciative smile.

"I'm ready for tea," Annie said. "Does anyone want another cup?" She ignored her mother's pleased look.

"I'll have another," Ike said.

When he entered the Zook farmhouse, Jacob heard Annie's laughter coming from the kitchen. Enjoying the delightful sound, he made his way toward the back of the house. Whenever he wasn't with her, he missed her. He anticipated her smile, longed for her response the next time he held her more properly in his arms and kissed her.

"Gut morning!" he said with a smile as he entered the kitchen. He became the focus of four pairs of eyes. He stopped abruptly. He was surprised to see Ike King

seated next to Annie at the table. His chest tightened. He nodded at Ike. *"Hallo."*

"Jacob." At least Horseshoe Joe looked pleased to see him. "Are you hungry?"

"Nay, but I'll take a glass of water." He sought Miriam's permission. "May I?"

She smiled. *"Ja,* of course."

Annie started to rise. "I'll get it."

Jacob held up his hand to stop her. "I know where everything is." The conversation resumed behind him as he reached into a kitchen cabinet and withdrew a glass. He filled the tumbler with water from the faucet. When he was done, he turned and leaned back against the cabinet as he lifted the glass to his lips. He took note of the gathering, his attention returning to Annie often.

"This is delicious," Ike said after he'd taken a bite of a cinnamon bun.

Annie avoided his glance. "That's kind of you to say."

"Annie is a wonderful cook," Jacob said pleasantly, trying to draw her attention. "Everything she makes comes out perfectly. You should taste her homemade bread."

Jacob was amused when her eyes shot daggers at him. "Not only is she a *gut* cook but she is modest about it. She will make some lucky man a fine wife." He couldn't help stirring things up a bit. Annie was livid, but Ike appeared pleased. Annie was angry, so she couldn't be indifferent to him.

"I get coffee and breakfast from her whenever I come to work—at least most of the time. Annie doesn't always know whether or not I'm working."

Ike looked concerned. "That's right. You injured your hand. Is it better?"

Jacob captured Annie's gaze and fought to keep it.

"My hand is healing," he said. He drank the last of the water and then set the glass in the dish basin. "I should get back." He turned to Annie. "We need to talk later."

"You'll be coming for lunch?" Joe asked, speaking up after being unusually quiet.

"*Danki*, but *nay*. I'll finish in the shop and then head home." He crossed the room to the nearest exit. "I'll see you on Sunday if not before. Miriam, *Mam* said to tell you that she'll bring roast beef on Sunday." This Sunday was visiting day. Friends and family would gather at the Zooks for a meal and conversation. The children—young and old—would play games outside as long as the weather held and didn't suddenly turn cold.

Jacob heard his pulse pounding in his ears as he left the house and continued toward the shop. What if Annie decided to marry Ike King? She certainly looked cozy seated next to him at the kitchen table. He suddenly felt unsure. Annie's anger with him could be just that—anger.

He released a shuddering breath. The memory of her and Ike's shared laughter stung. Seeing them together made his chest tighten and his thoughts churn.

If Ike is the man you want, Annie Zook, then I wish you well.

"*Jacob!*" Annie came out of the house and approached him. With heart beating hard, he waited for her.

When he saw the look on her face, he raised an eyebrow. "*Ja?*"

She scowled up at him. "What was that about?"

He regarded her with amusement. "What was what about?"

"You know. You were playing matchmaker, telling Ike that I'd make some man a wonderful wife. Why? You know I hate that."

He saw her eyes fill and his heart gave a lurch, although he knew her tears were of anger, not sadness. "You wanted a man like Ike to wed. I thought I'd help by telling the truth."

"By trying to sell me with fancy words and too much praise for my cooking?" she challenged.

"Annie—"

"I didn't appreciate it, Jacob. If I'm meant to marry Ike, then it will be God's will and mine. Not *Mam's* and yours!" She turned then and stomped toward the house.

"Annie!" he called out. She froze in her tracks but didn't turn around. "'Tis *not* my will that you marry Ike," he told her.

She turned and stared at him. "What *do* you want, Jacob?" The memory of their shared kiss hung in the air between them. When he didn't immediately answer, Annie sighed. "I should get back."

Watching her leave, he felt an overwhelming surge of love. She was always beautiful to him, but she never looked more so than with fire in her blue eyes and her hands planted firmly on her hips. He wanted to follow her, take her into his arms and kiss her until she was breathless.

"Annie!" he called as she climbed the porch steps, but she didn't stop. She disappeared inside, leaving him yearning for her company and her love, and regretting that he'd kissed her, then stayed away.

Jacob returned to the shop and went to work, but he had trouble concentrating. After dropping the hot piece of metal three times, he set the unfinished object on the worktable and put away his tools. Then he left the shop and Horseshoe Joe's farm. He needed to think, to put distance between him and Annie Zook—and quickly.

Chapter Fifteen

❧

"Annie, did you wash the kitchen curtains?" *Mam* asked the following Friday.

"*Ja, Mam*. And hung them on the line." Annie smiled. "And I dusted all of the furniture, and Barbara did the floors," she said, anticipating her mother's next question. Her mother and sister and she were preparing for this visiting Sunday's company.

Annie could tell that her mother was running a list of chores through her mind. She approached, put a hand on her shoulder. "*Mam*, what's wrong? You know that we're always more than ready whenever we host visiting Sunday. It's not as if our entire church community will be visiting. Only some of our closest friends and neighbors."

Mam sighed and rubbed a hand across her eyes. She appeared worried as she met Annie's gaze. "I'm concerned about your *grossmudder*. She hasn't been herself again lately. Earlier this morning, she fell."

Annie became alarmed. "Did she hurt herself?"

"She's bruised and sore. I fear she is failing again." *Mam* captured Annie's hand with her own. "I think she needs to see a doctor."

An *Englisher*, Annie thought. After her father's accident, her mother would be as worried about the expense of the doctor's visit as she was concerned about *Grossmudder's* health.

"Things will be fine," she told her mother. "The Lord will watch over *Grossmudder* and all of us."

Mam's expression softened. "Annie, you are a joy to me," she said. "All of you *kinner* are." She squeezed Annie's hand and then released it. "But you have been the strength in this family since your *vadder's* accident. I shudder to think what might have happened if not for your quick thinking after he fell."

Annie waved away the praise. "I ran for help. It was Jacob Lapp who got *Dat* the help he needed." *Jacob.* She hadn't seen him since he'd come into the house when Ike King had stopped by to return her mother's soup bowl. Had he worked in the shop yesterday?

Did she care? In truth, she was still angry with him. He had embarrassed her in front of Ike, much as her mother had done with Joseph, Levi and Reuben. And he'd kissed her simply because she was there and available. That's what hurt the most. That he could so easily play with her emotions and then dismiss her.

Anger is a sin. She said a silent prayer, asking for the Lord's forgiveness, seeking His guidance with Jacob.

Her thoughts turned to Barbara and Levi. She and Barbara had encountered Levi in town when they'd run an errand for *Mam*. She had made all of the purchases while her sister and Levi had spent a few precious moments together. Recalling her sister's expression during the ride home, Annie grinned.

Her mother, she realized, was studying her carefully. "Why are you grinning?"

"Barbara and I saw Levi Stoltzfus in the store yesterday. I'm remembering how happy Barbara looked on the way home."

Mam looked pleased. "Levi is *gut* for your sister."

Annie nodded. *And me? Who is the man for me?* "About *Grossmudder*, I think we should bring her here."

"She'll want to clean *haus* with us," *Mam* warned as she rubbed her temple.

"The *haus* is clean," she reminded her. "She can arrange the desserts on plates for us."

Her mother smiled. "That's a wonderful idea." She paused. "Annie—" *Mam* added as Annie opened the back screen door.

She halted and faced her. *"Ja, Mam?"*

"Jacob Lapp is a *fine, young* man," her mother said, surprising her.

"He's been *kind* to all of us."

"And you especially," she said softly.

Annie felt a flash of heat. "He's just a friend."

"Ja. A friend." Her brow furrowed as *Mam* looked contemplative.

Annie sensed her concern. *"Ja,* he is." *Was*, she thought. And she was foolish enough to want him to be more. She released a breath. "Ike King will be coming tomorrow. He, too, is a *gut* man."

"It was kind of him to return my soup bowl before Sunday," *Mam* said.

"Ja," Annie agreed as she continued on. "I'll be right back with *Grossmudder.*"

As she walked the distance between the main farmhouse and the *dawdi haus*, Annie thought of Jacob Lapp. Her mother suspected that there might be something more than friendship between her and Jacob. How wrong could she be? Jacob had been right when he'd told her that her mother wouldn't approve of him as anything more than her friend. *Mam* saw Jacob only as a man without the financial means to support a wife and family.

Annie swallowed hard. He had asked if she trusted him. She had trusted him, but no more. He had played with her affections and then…nothing.

If only things were different… She released a small sob as she reached the *grosseldre's* house. Annie paused on the front steps to wipe her eyes. After several deep breaths, she stood up straight, then knocked on her *grossmudder's* door.

"Annie says she likes Ike, but I'm beginning to think she prefers Jacob." Miriam Zook looked worried as she confided in her husband.

Horseshoe Joe shrugged. "What's wrong with Jacob?" He rose from his chair and noted that his previously injured leg felt stronger. "Jake is a *hard-working, young* man who loves our daughter, and Ike— Well, he is a kind man, but he is too old for Annie."

"But she wants an older husband." His wife reached out to steady him.

Joe shook his head. "I need to learn to get around on my own, Miriam." When his wife nodded and stepped back as if stung, Joe softened his expression and his tone. "'Tis not that I don't need you, but I need to do this by myself." He gazed at her lovingly. There was no one else in the house at the moment, a rare thing when parents had teenage and older children who lived with them.

Miriam smiled and walked with him as he hobbled to the kitchen.

"Does Annie really want an older man? Or does she want young Jacob?" Joe asked as they entered the room. "She can't want both."

"She needs someone who can take care of her." She

put the coffeepot on the stove to heat. "Jacob cannot provide for her."

Joe lowered himself gingerly into a kitchen chair and watched her work. "You underestimate him, Miriam. He is a Lapp, after all."

She set out two cups and waited by the table for the coffee to percolate. "Ike has a *haus* and farmland, and he needs a wife and a family. Annie would be *gut* for him," she insisted.

Joe grabbed her arm as she moved toward the counter. "But will Ike be *gut* for Annie? Would she truly be happy as his wife?" He released her and she stared at him. "She doesn't look at Ike the way you gaze at me, dearest."

She scowled, although she seemed pleased by his endearment. "She will learn to love him." She reached for the sugar and then fetched the cream from the refrigerator.

"And that is what you want for her? Someone she must *learn* to love?" He sighed. "Annie is afraid to love. Whether or not the man is older makes no difference. If she loves again, she will be hurt if things don't work out as they should."

"What would you have me do?" she asked.

"Allow things to take their natural course. If Annie is meant to be with Ike, then so shall she be. If she wants Jacob, then let God's will be done."

As his wife poured his coffee, Joe hoped that Miriam would stop interfering in his middle daughter's love life. Jacob had become a fine man, and Joe loved him as one of his own. He'd cautioned his wife about playing matchmaker to any of their children, but that didn't mean he couldn't ask the Lord for a little help. Jacob and Annie had barely spoken to each other. That had to change soon.

While he drank his coffee and enjoyed time alone

with his wife, Joe pushed an idea to the back of his mind. Later, after supper, Joe stepped outside for a breath of fresh air. Soon, the winter weather would set in, and they would be locked inside the warmth of the house except for those times when farm chores drove them into the bitter cold.

November was the month of weddings. He would enjoy seeing Annie happily wed, but to only one man. Jacob Lapp.

His leg pained him, a sure sign that it was going to rain or that a full moon was imminent. Joe moved from the porch railing and limped over to sit on a rocker. *Weather is about to change*, he thought.

"Lord, what do You think?" he said. "Could You help me make two young people happy?"

Joe knew with certainty that Jacob Lapp was in love with Annie, despite the fact that Jacob had gone out of his way to avoid her in recent days. And somehow he knew that Annie loved Jake, despite her willingness to spend time with Ike King.

When it came down to it, if Ike proposed, would Annie accept and follow through?

Joe put it all in God's hands.

On Sunday morning, Annie came out of the house as the first visitors arrived. She smiled at her father, who sat on a porch rocker watching as a buggy pulled into the yard. "'Tis a lovely day," she said.

"*Ja.* Hope the weather holds out. Hard to tell with the way this leg is hurting me."

Annie frowned. "Do you need a pain pill?"

"You know I don't like to take pills. I had to after the surgery, but this—" He rubbed along the area of the re-paired bone. "I can deal with this ache. Might have to learn to live with it. Only the Lord knows if it will fade in time."

"Dat," Annie said with concern, "it will get better, I'm sure of it."

Joe regarded her with affection as he reached over to pet Millie, who rested near his chair. "If you're sure of it, then I believe." He jerked his head in the direction of the Hershbergers—Annie's aunt and cousins—who had left their buggy and were approaching the house. "You'd best put Millie upstairs," he said, and Annie hurried to obey, returning in time to greet her aunt and cousins.

Her Aunt Alta was a *gut* soul, but at times, she could be trying, Annie thought. She didn't always think before she spoke and when that happened, someone's feelings were often unintentionally hurt.

"Alta," *Dat* greeted as Annie waved her cousins inside. Neither daughter was wed or being courted. Annie wondered with amusement if the men who liked her cousins feared having Alta as a mother-in-law. "*Mam* has tea and coffee ready. Would you like a cup?"

"I'll have coffee," Mary said.

"Make that two," Sally replied.

Annie looked at her cousins and thought how much they resembled their mother, as Alta might have been when, as a young girl, she'd fallen in love with *Mam's* brother John. From what her *grossmudder* told her, Alta's love for John had made her breathtakingly lovely in her joy. But after John died tragically at the young age of twenty-eight, Alta had been devastated. She had gone into mourning, from which she nearly hadn't emerged. It was only the fact that her two fatherless daughters had desperately needed her that Alta had pulled herself from the depths of despair and gone on to care for them with love and affection. The loss of her husband had stolen something vital in Alta's life. She had not remarried and had become a busybody, eager to gossip about neighbors and friends. The nattering wasn't malicious, not intentionally, Annie thought, but everyone knew not to tell Alta anything in confidence.

Annie smiled inwardly as she gave coffee to each of her cousins. On the other hand, if there was news that someone was eager to share, Alta was the one to tell, for then everyone in Happiness would know within forty-eight hours.

"Do you know who's coming today?" Mary asked. She sipped from her coffee as she waited for Annie's reply.

"The Kings, the Lapps and the Bylers," Annie began. "*Ach*, and the Masts and the Troyers." Annie tried to think of who else had promised to visit, but couldn't recall.

"Will the preacher come?" Sally asked.

"*Ja.*" Of that, Annie had no doubt, especially when she thought of the last time she'd seen Barbara and Levi Stoltzfus together. She didn't believe that Levi would pass up an opportunity to spend time with her sister.

"Why don't we go outside while the weather is still warm?" Annie suggested.

After agreeing, Sally and Mary took their coffee and followed Annie out onto the covered front porch. A large family buggy had parked next to the Hershbergers, and Abram and Charlotte Peachy along with their children stepped out.

"*Ach, ja!*" Annie exclaimed. "And the Abram Peachys."

Sally grinned. "Obviously."

Another gray buggy pulled up in the yard. "Isn't that Ike King?" Mary said.

Annie nodded when the kind man took notice of her

and waved. "Excuse me, cousins," she said, forcing herself to greet him with a smile. "*Hallo*, Ike."

Samuel Lapp drove his family buggy down the dirt lane toward the Joseph Zook farmhouse. "Do we have everyone?"

"A little late to ask, don't ya think, *Dat*?" Eli sounded amused. "We're already here."

As his mother and siblings chuckled, Jacob exchanged smiles with his twin brother. His amusement promptly faded as he recalled seeing Annie with Ike King, laughing and talking in Miriam's kitchen the other day. Seeing Ike sitting so comfortably at the table had made him realize that Annie might have found her match.

The teasing comments between his family members continued, but Jacob was lost in his own thoughts. Eli tapped him on the shoulder through the open window. Jacob was surprised to realize that everyone had left the vehicle except him.

Eli eyed him with a frown. "What is wrong?"

Jacob shook his head. "I shouldn't be here."

"Annie." His brother sighed. "I told you it was dangerous for you to be in her company. You love her, and now you're hurting. What has she done now?"

He paused. "She's decided on Ike King."

Eli raised his eyebrows. "Amos's brother?" He gestured toward the door, reminding Jacob that he needed to get out of the buggy.

Jacob took the hint and climbed down. "*Ja*, Amos's brother. A *widower*."

"I find it difficult to believe." Eli started toward the house, and reluctantly, Jacob fell into step with him.

"Believe it," Jacob said. "I've seen them together— more than once."

Eli shrugged. "You've seen me with Mary Hershberger, and there is nothing between us."

Jacob felt as if his feet were made of lead as he continued on. "Mary is not interested in you. She likes Joseph Byler, and you know that. Ike *is* interested in Annie Zook, and Annie seems to be comfortable with him. She wants to marry an older man."

Eli was shaking his head. "*Nay*, I think not."

"You wait and see for yourself," Jacob challenged him. "I know Annie Zook."

"How often have you seen her since you hurt your hand?" Eli asked.

"The past couple of times I worked, she never once came out to talk or visit."

"You haven't exactly encouraged her."

Jacob readjusted his hat. "I kissed her."

"You *what*?"

"It happened after the singing. The time seemed right, but then it all went wrong."

"What did she say afterward?" Eli asked.

Jacob frowned. "Nothing. We didn't have a chance to discuss it."

"You kissed her and then stayed away? That was foolish, Jake." His twin knew him too well.

"I know." He spied a group of men in the side yard and switched directions. Eli followed his lead. "But it's too late now."

"Is it? You love this woman, but you avoid her after one kiss. What are you waiting for? To be miserable after she marries someone else?"

The thought of Annie marrying Ike made Jacob sick inside. "I can't tell her. I missed my chance." He felt as if he were twelve again and heartbroken after having learned that Annie was in love with Jedidiah, his eldest brother. "If I'm wrong about her feelings for Ike, I'll know soon enough and then I'll tell her how I feel. If I'm right, I'll keep my distance. I want her to be happy, even if it means losing her."

"You're a fool, Jacob."

A fool for Annie, Jacob thought. "Wait until you fall in love, Eli. Until then, don't judge me."

Eli halted, put a hand on Jacob's shoulder. "I'm not judging you, Jake. I want you to be happy with her. It frustrates me that you won't do anything, and I can't help you."

Jacob gave him a wry smile. "I'm sorry, Eli. I'm not myself."

"*Ja*, you are, and I admire you for it. You think I don't want a wife of my own? A home? A family? I want all of those things, but I'm not ready yet."

"When you meet the right woman, you'll be ready," Jacob said with conviction.

His brother grinned at him. "Then what are *you* waiting for?"

As they joined the men, the back door to the farm-house opened and Annie Zook stepped outside with Ike King. Jacob elbowed his brother, nodded in the couple's direction.

Eli frowned. "Maybe it's not as it seems."

Jacob felt a burning in his stomach. "And maybe it is." He couldn't tear his gaze away. Annie happened to glance over in his direction, and their gazes locked a moment before she looked away.

"There's *Dat*," Eli said, grabbing hold of his arm. "Let's join him and the others. It looks like we'll be dining outside today since the weather has taken a delightful turn."

He knew his brother was trying to distract him. Jacob

tore his gaze away, feeling battered and bruised. His heart was aching. How could he have allowed it to happen?

Because love just happens. Love was a gift from God, which should be cherished for all the small, memorable moments he'd enjoyed with Annie, even if he wasn't meant to have her for a lifetime, as his wife.

"Come on, Jake," Eli urged.

He hadn't realized that he'd hesitated. Jacob nodded and continued on.

Eli looked at him with concern. "You will find some other woman to make you happy."

But would he? Jacob didn't think so. He believed he'd never love anyone as much as he loved Annie. If he didn't act now, he would lose all hope of having her. He had to do something, but what?

Chapter Sixteen

"I'd like to take you around my property sometime," Ike said as he accompanied Annie outside. "Show you my *haus*. You've seen the kitchen. I'd like you to see the rest of it."

Annie looked at him. "And Barbara?

His hesitation was barely visible, but Annie noticed. "*Ja*, Barbara, too." He softened his tone. "But it is *you* I want to have see everything."

Ike's words gave her a jolt. The man apparently was interested in her, and she should be happy, for he was the kind of man who would make her a good husband, yet...

Her thoughts turned to Jacob Lapp. Could she settle for Ike if her heart belonged to Jacob? Ike was still talking, telling her about all the things he wanted her to see. Annie nodded, smiled and barely heard him as she looked over at Jacob, who had captured her attention. Jacob Lapp walked with his brother Eli toward the gathering of men. He turned and they locked gazes. Annie felt a rush of heat. Embarrassed to be caught staring, she could only imagine the look in the man's bright eyes.

"And I wanted your opinion on a new mare I purchased…" Ike said, but Annie was distracted by Jacob. "…I know you will have much to do in the *haus*."

Annie stiffened. "I will have to check with *Mam*," she said, "I have my chores to do."

Ike looked puzzled. "*Ja*. I know you do a lot in your family's *haus*. I wouldn't ask you to neglect your chores." He regarded her closely and frowned. "Annie, aren't you well?"

She felt an overwhelming burst of relief. He hadn't been talking about her working in *his* house. If that was the case, then she would have panicked—it would have been happening all too soon.

She saw Jacob and Eli Lapp had joined the men. Her heart skipped a beat. Jacob was deep in conversation with his father and brother. Abram Peachy and Amos King, Abram's father-in-law and Ike's brother, approached and joined in the conversation.

As if following the direction of her gaze, Ike said, "I'll leave you to the women. I will visit with the men."

Annie nodded, relieved to see him go, when only a short while ago, she'd been glad to welcome him. She should be enjoying every moment spent in Ike's company, but she found herself distracted, her thoughts returning again and again to the younger man with dark hair and golden eyes, the man who had kissed her and made her fall in love.

"Annie!" her mother's voice called from the doorway.

"Coming, *Mam*!" She ran inside, glad to have something to do to take her mind off Ike King and Jacob Lapp. Why couldn't she stop thinking of Jacob when her goal of finding an older sweetheart was within reach?

The kitchen was filled with women as Annie stepped into the room.

"I thought we could eat outside," *Mam* told her, "but

your *dat's* leg has been hurting." She smiled. "He's become a *gut* weather forecaster. He said it will rain or there will be a full moon."

"Ja," Aunt Alta said, "my hip has been bothering me. It will rain."

Annie greeted the women. When she approached Charlotte, the young woman smiled and introduced Martha Schrock, her brother-in-law Eli's cousin.

"She has come to visit from Indiana," Charlotte said.

Annie smiled and welcomed Martha, a dark-haired, unmarried woman in her mid-twenties. She was a plain woman without a husband, according to Aunt Alta. *Will I be like her if I don't marry Ike?* "You're staying with Sarah and Eli."

"Ja," Martha said. "I haven't seen Eli since he was a boy. I am enjoying my time here."

As she carried on a conversation with the woman, Annie recognized God's light in her. She might be plain, but there was something about her brown eyes, her warm smile and her ability to listen. Martha looked and paid attention to her as if she were the only one in the room.

"I'm glad you could be here today," Annie said.

"Danki," Martha replied.

When her mother called to her from the gathering room, Annie gave Martha a look of apology. "Coming," she called. "No doubt she wants me to set up a table so we can put out the food."

"May I help?" Martha seemed eager for something to do.

"That would be wonderful." Annie entered the room with Martha.

"There you are," *Mam* said. *"Gut. Hallo*, Martha, have you come to help?"

Martha nodded, and Annie's mother quickly instructed

where she wanted the furniture arranged. With Martha's help, Annie shifted a table to another area of the room. "I hope it is not too heavy."

Martha smiled. *"Nay."* After they set it down, the woman held up her hands. They were large hands for a woman, and clearly she had done her share of hard work.

"Let's get the other one," Annie said.

Martha nodded. When the tables were in their proper place, according to *Mam*, Annie smiled and said, "Let's get something to drink before we put out the food." Martha agreed as she trailed her back into the kitchen.

Annie and the other women had put out all the food when the men arrived to eat first, as was custom on Sundays. If they had chosen to dine outside, then families might have sat down together. They had shared tables on Church and visiting Sundays before. It was up to the preacher, and since Levi Stoltzfus said nothing about relaxing the custom this Sunday, Annie, Martha and the other women, along with the children, waited for their turn.

Annie became aware of Jacob as he entered the room. He captured her gaze as he walked by. "Annie," he said, but Annie noticed that he didn't smile.

She felt a tightening in her throat as she whispered, "Jacob."

Ike King, on the other hand, grinned at her as he passed by her to take his seat. Conscious of Jacob and Ike, Annie left the gathering room with its makeshift bench tables and bench seats. In the kitchen, Katie Lapp and her two daughters-in-law, Sarah and Rachel, were enjoying a cup of tea while they waited for the men to finish.

"I prefer it when we all eat together," Katie said, and the other women agreed.

Jacob's young sister, Hannah, burst into the kitchen. She and the other children had been outside, playing in the yard. "*Mam*, is it almost time to eat?"

"*Ja*, Hannah, but you must be patient," Katie said. She glanced past her daughter to the window. "Where are your *bruders*?"

"Daniel and Isaac are inside with *Dat*," she said. "Joseph is outside with me."

Katie's lips twitched. "Will you tell Joseph to come inside?"

Hannah's golden head nodded vigorously.

"Are Will and Elam outside?" Josie asked of her two young sons.

"*Ja*. I can get them, too," Hannah said.

Josie exchanged smiles with Katie as the child ran back to round up her playmates. "She is growing fast, Katie."

Annie agreed. She longed to have a child like Hannah, wanted to have a large number of them.

Her thoughts returned to Ike and Jacob. Ike liked her. Should she allow him to court her if he asked?

It was Jacob who made her feel alive. She imagined him holding their child, and pictured him running in the yard, chasing their *kinner*. The image was wonderful—and out of her reach. What was she doing with Ike King?

She frowned. *Because I don't know what Jacob's intentions are?*

Her mother broke into her thoughts. "Annie, would you check to see if your *dat* or any of the men need anything?"

"*Ja, Mam.*" Annie headed toward the gathering room, thoughts of Jacob whirling in her head.

"Do *ya* mind if I come?" Martha asked shyly.

"Not at all." Annie moved aside to allow her room.

The men had finished eating and were starting to rise from the tables.

"Is there anything else you need?" Annie asked. "Dessert? Or would you like it later?" Most of the men chose to wait.

Ike King approached with a smile. "Annie, the meal was delicious."

"I'm glad you enjoyed it." Annie felt slightly uncomfortable with his praise. She pulled Martha forward and introduced her. "She's Eli Schrock's cousin."

Ike inclined his head and offered her a smile. "*Hallo.* A pleasure to meet you."

Martha beamed.

Annie left Ike and Martha to talk, and moved to pick up dishes and plates and ready the dining area for the women and younger children.

She was engrossed in the task and didn't realize that someone had approached from behind. Then she felt an odd tingling at the base of her neck, and she turned. Jacob Lapp stood a few feet away, watching her.

"Jacob!" she gasped.

"Annie." His voice was quiet, his expression unreadable. "Are you angry with me?"

She stilled for a moment, then shook her head.

He raised an eyebrow. "I saw you with Ike again." He gave her a crooked smile. "Are you going to marry him?"

Annie felt flustered. She loved Jacob and fought to hide it. She wanted to tell him, but she was afraid. She'd never felt this way before—not with Jedidiah and certainly not with Ike. "Ike is a nice man."

Jacob nodded. He turned toward a window to watch the children playing in the yard. Annie couldn't keep her eyes off him. The sight of him stole her breath. He wore his Sunday best and his long-sleeved white shirt emphasized his arms, reminding her of the way they moved as he worked in her father's shop. He was taller than her, but not too tall. She couldn't tell by his features what he was thinking.

"Ike is kind," Jacob finally said. He hesitated, turned from the window to face her. "But is he truly the man for you?"

She looked down, afraid to answer him lest he see the truth of her feelings for him in her eyes. Her attention focused on his injured hand. The burned area was healed but still red. "Your burn looks better." She had the strong urge to gently take hold of his hand, smooth her finger over the scar. When Jacob didn't answer, Annie looked up and found him studying her curiously. His intense gaze gave her goose bumps. "Do I have a mark on my nose?" she asked.

His lips twitched. *"Nay."* His gaze caressed her face. "You didn't answer my question about Ike."

She raised her chin. "And I'm not going to."

He sighed and glanced out the window. "I should go. Eli is waiting for me." He faced her. "Annie, I want you to know that I am happy for you. I wish you and Ike all the best," he said.

Nay, she cried silently. *I don't want Ike. I want you!* Her sister had said, *Why don't you tell him?* Barbara was right. What did she have to lose?

"Jacob!" He was at the door when she called out. He stopped and turned, his expression closed off. She shook her head, afraid to continue. There were others around; this wasn't the time or place. "I will call you when dessert is ready."

His brow cleared, but his expression didn't soften. He continued outside to join his brother, and Annie watched him with tears in her eyes but made no attempt to stop him. She crossed through the house to the front porch. Her father was seated on a rocker, rubbing his sore leg.

"*Dat*, what are you doing out here by yourself?"

He gestured for her to sit on the rocking chair next to his. "I needed to rest this leg." He looked at the clear sky. "I still think it's going to rain." He turned back to her, and Annie blushed. Could he tell she'd been crying? Would he ask why?

If he'd noticed, he didn't say as he gazed out over the barnyard. "Can I get you anything?"

"*Nay.*" He sighed.

Jacob and Eli came into their line of vision as they walked to their buggy. Watching Jacob, Annie drew a sharp breath. She sensed when her father looked at her, and she smiled as she faced him. He didn't need to know that she'd foolishly fallen in love with Jacob Lapp.

She pretended indifference as Jacob stood near the family buggy while Eli reached into the back and pulled out a ball. Eli held it up and shouted. Suddenly, a group of children came barreling toward him from the side yard.

Eli laughed and ran while calling out to his twin. He tossed the ball to Jacob, and as he reached for it, Jacob fell. The children piled on top of him. Annie gasped, but her father only chuckled. Soon, children were tossed this way and that as Jacob rose with ball still clutched under his arm.

There were shouts of glee and laughter as the children chased Jacob around the yard. He shouted for his older brother Noah to join in. Soon, all the older Lapp siblings were involved in playing catch over the children's heads. Jacob caught the ball and pretended to drop it. When his youngest brother Joseph grabbed it, Jacob picked up the little boy and threatened to toss Joseph with the

ball while he ran. The little boy's giggles were sweet to
Annie's ears.

Annie smiled as she watched them. Seeing Jacob having fun with the children, hearing his laughter made her
think of things she wanted but couldn't have. Jacob as
her husband playing with their children, flashing her
smiles of love and joy whenever he glanced toward her,
which was often.

Disturbed by her thoughts, she concentrated on the
good time before her. She laughed at some of Jacob's
antics, gasped when a group of youngsters shoved him
to the ground.

"They are having fun," Joe said. "If it wasn't for this
leg, I'd join them."

Annie looked at him with surprise. "You would?"

Joe nodded. *"Ja."* He paused as if choosing his words
carefully, "Annie, Ike King—"

She stiffened. "What about him?"

"He's headed this way." *Dat* held her glance. "There is
something I need to show you in the shop. Do you want
to talk with him first?"

"Now?" she asked with raised eyebrows.

"Ja." Her father rose and reached for his cane. "But
we can go later if you need time with Ike."

Annie noted Ike's purposeful strides as he crossed the
yard. She didn't particularly want to talk with him right
now. She met her father's gaze. "I'll go with you." Her
father looked pleased. "I'll tell *Mam.*"

Dat shook his head. *"Nay*, no need. She's busy with
her friends." He rose and took several steps on his sore
leg, grimacing with each one.

"Wait here," she told him.

"Annie—"

"I'll be right back." She hurried inside for his wheelchair. When she returned, she found her father talking with Ike.

Looking pleased at her approach, Ike smiled. "I told your *dat* about our scheduled ride through my property."

Had they scheduled a ride? Annie glanced from Ike to her father, then back to Ike. Her father's expression hid his thoughts. "Ike, *Dat* needs me right now," she said. "Can we talk later?"

Ike blinked. "*Ja*, of course." Then he smiled. "When you are done, come and find me."

"Why did you bring that?" *Dat* asked of the wheel-chair.

Annie maneuvered the chair so that he could sit down. "You're in pain, and I thought you should rest your leg awhile longer."

Without argument, he sat in the wheelchair. "Let's go before someone else delays us. I want to get back in time to watch the children play horseshoes."

Annie noted the game's pegs some distance away from each other on the lawn. She pushed her father across the yard until they reached the shop, where she left the wheelchair to open the door. When she returned to guide him inside, her father raised a hand to stop her. "I can manage," he said. He pushed himself into the smithy.

"Would you please open up the back window? The day is nice enough, and for now there is plenty of light."

Annie obeyed, then waited for further instructions.

Her father gestured toward a shelf. "The notebook. Would you get it for me?"

Annie reached for the book and silently handed it to him. "Is something wrong?

"*Nay*, daughter." He opened the book and smiled up at her. "Everything is right. Come around. I want to show you this."

Annie frowned as she shifted to his side. "What is it?"

"A listing of all the work that Jacob has done while I've been recovering. Since he stepped in to help, business at the blacksmithy has been better than ever."

At the mention of Jacob, Annie felt warmth skitter across her skin. "He has done well for you. That is *gut*," she said, trying not to give away her thoughts.

"*Ja.* So well that I am going to ask him if he will stay and work with me. Jacob seems to enjoy it, and I like having him here."

Annie struggled to hide a rush of heat brought on by his name. "You want him to work here permanently?"

Her father watched her closely. "*Ja.*" He gestured about the shop. "It looks organized, doesn't it? He leaves it as neat as a pin when he's done. I like that. And the business is profitable. Josiah has never been interested in blacksmithing. And Peter? It's hard to tell, but Jacob— he wanted to learn from early on."

Feeling restless, Annie wandered about, touching tools and work spaces—the table, vise and anvil. Everywhere she looked, she saw not only her father working here but now Jacob, moving about the shop, working with fire and metal.

"Have you asked him yet?" she said, feeling shaky.

"*Nay.*" He smiled. "I wanted your opinion first."

Annie widened her gaze. "Mine? Why?"

"I value your judgment."

She was so stunned she couldn't answer him. It was unusual that a father would value his daughter's thoughts. She was pleased that he felt this way. She considered her father's decision. If *Dat* believed that Jacob should stay on, then who was she to say *nay*?

"If you think Jacob should stay, then I think he should," she said.

Her father sighed and maneuvered himself out of the chair, grimaced then sat again. "Annie."

"Ja, Dat?"

"Ike King is interested in you. I believe he sees you as his future wife."

"He's a nice man," she said carefully.

"But do you want to marry him?"

Annie didn't want to answer, but she knew she must. "He is the kind of man I'd hoped to marry."

"So you will agree to become his wife?"

Annie opened her mouth and then closed it. She thought of her love for Jacob, and she began to cry. "Why is this so hard? Ike is the man I *should* marry, but—"

"You're in love with Jacob Lapp," her father said quietly.

Startled, she stared at him. *"Ja,"* she whispered. "Is my love for him that obvious?" She sniffed and wiped her eyes. *"Dat,* how can I continue to love a man who has no interest in me? I thought if I avoided handsome men, I'd be safe, but I can't help loving Jacob—"

Her father smiled and patted her arm. "There is nothing wrong with loving Jacob."

She nodded, her eyes overflowing. "Except that he doesn't return my love. It's like Jed all over again. Will I ever learn? Only I love Jacob more than anything, more than I ever loved Jedidiah."

"Why not tell him?" *Dat* asked.

"Nay! I can't. I don't want to be hurt again. And it is not up to a woman to tell a man she loves him…not when he hasn't told her of his love."

Her father sighed. "You and Jacob are both stubborn as mules." He rose from his wheelchair and hobbled over to a wall cabinet where he kept supplies and specially crafted tools. Stretching to the top shelf with a loud groan, he grabbed something and took it down.

"Here," he said as he extended the metal box to her.

"What is it?"

"Take a look."

Annie took the box out of her father's hands. She turned to study it from every side. "It looks like it was made in the shop." Baffled, she met her *dat's* gaze. "It's pretty. Why did you want me to see it?"

The container was crudely made but there was something endearing about it. It was lovely but it didn't appear to have been made by him recently. She softened her expression. "You made this for *Mam* when you were younger?" She felt warmth inside at the love her father must have felt for her mother at such a young age to have made such a gift.

"*Nay*. Take a look on the bottom," her father instructed.

Annie carefully turned it over, saw that something had been scratched into the surface—"Jacob and Annie," inside the shape of a heart.

Annie felt an overwhelming rush of feeling. "Jacob made this for me?" she whispered.

Her father smiled. "*Ja*. When he was younger. Jacob made that during the months he worked in the shop with me."

Annie clutched the box to her breast. "I don't understand."

"How can you marry Ike when you love Jacob?"

Tears filling her eyes again, Annie shook her head. "I can't. How can I marry without love?" she sobbed. "I love Jacob, but I don't know how he really feels about me." She drew a shuddering breath. "I thought that maybe he cared, but then…something happened." *His kiss.* "And suddenly he was avoiding me. He once asked if I trusted him, and I did, but then he changed, and I didn't know what to think."

"Jacob is trustworthy. Why don't you talk with him?" her father said. "Show him the box. See what he says." He captured her hand. "Maybe he is as unsure of you as you are of him. Annie, don't wait. Do it now."

Should she risk all and talk with him? What if he didn't love her? *What if he does?* She'd be foolish if she did nothing. "I'll talk with him," she promised.

"Thanks be to God," she thought she heard her father murmur as she left the shop.

Chapter Seventeen

Annie saw Jacob purposefully striding in her direction as she exited the barn into the autumn sunshine. She saw his determined look and grew concerned.

"Annie!" he called as he crossed the yard. "We need to talk!"

She lifted a hand and waved. "Jacob!"

She heard a child's wild cry and saw a horseshoe flying toward Jacob. It happened so fast there was nothing she could do but watch as the curved piece of metal connected with the back of Jacob's head. The thud against his flesh propelled her forward. She screamed and ran to him.

"Jacob!" Crouching beside him, she cupped his face. "Jacob? Talk to me. Are you all right?" She leaned closer, felt his breath fan her cheek and knew the tiniest bit of relief.

"Jacob," she urged, "you're scaring me. We do need to talk."

His eyelashes flickered.

"Annie." Eli stood behind her. "Is he all right?"

She looked up with tears in her eyes. "I don't know! He has to be! There is something important I need to tell him, that I love him—" She glanced back as Jacob's eyes opened. He moaned softly and attempted to sit up. She reached to help him, feeling the strength of muscle beneath his shirtsleeve.

"I'm all right." Upright now, he grabbed her hand. "What do you need to tell me?" he asked hoarsely.

Feeling suddenly shy, Annie stood. Grabbing the box from the ground, she hid it against her back. What if her father was wrong?

But what if he was right?

"Eli," she heard him say, "help me up. Annie and I have to talk."

Annie shot him a glance. "Jacob—"

He stood, grimacing, but there was a look in his glazed golden eyes that set her heart racing. Jacob held out his hand to her. "Walk with me," he said. She saw him studying her intently. His expression changed as if he'd read her face and liked what he saw.

"Jacob, we shouldn't. You're hurt." Nervous, she backed away.

"Annie, *please.*"

She saw the panic in his handsome face, and she relented and took his hand. As his fingers entwined with hers, she experienced a feeling of joy like no other. "Where do you want to go?" she asked huskily.

"Anywhere we can be alone."

Her heart skipped a beat. She nodded toward the fields. "We can walk the farm." She glanced over her shoulder. Her father had wheeled himself back to the gathering. They locked eyes, and she saw his pleased smile.

She and Jacob walked without talking for a time. The air felt thick with anticipation. Annie waited for Jacob to speak, and when he didn't, she wondered what to say.

"What are you carrying?" Jacob asked after a long moment of silence, referring to the object she had in her other hand.

Annie frowned, realized that she still held the box. She didn't want to pull away. She liked the feel of their hands touching. She stopped, faced him, let go of his hand, but she didn't immediately show him the box. "Jacob, the others will have plenty to say about us walking off alone together."

"Annie, tell me," he asked urgently. "Do you love me?" His golden eyes burned. "Enough to marry me? Or do you still want Ike?"

She inhaled sharply. *Marry him?* She closed her eyes and wondered if she was dreaming. "Jacob, I—"

"What is that behind your back?" His voice was soft, tender. "Show me." She was disarmed by his expression and quiet tone. "Annie?" He gazed at her with his beautiful tawny eyes in a face so handsome that he stole her breath.

She hesitated, then showed him the metal box.

Jacob looked stunned. "Where did you find that?"

"*Dat* gave it to me." His expression worried her. "He took it out of the shop cabinet."

She saw deep emotion contort his expression. "I thought I'd tossed it away."

"Jacob…" she began.

"*Nay,*" he said in a strangled voice. "Do you know what that is?" He turned and moved away.

Annie felt his pain as she crossed the distance between them. "It's a beautiful box," she whispered. "A gift from a young boy to a young girl, who had no idea how he felt about her." She was stunned by the knowledge that Jacob had spent hours as a youth, firing and hammering metal into this precious box for her. She placed a hand on his shoulder. She felt his tremor before he jerked away.

"I was young," he said bitterly, "and I adored you."

"Jacob—" Her heart tripped hard.

"And now you know how I feel."

Annie inhaled sharply. "I love you, Jacob," she whispered.

"Don't marry Ike, Annie. He can't make you happy." Jacob cupped her face. Holding her steady, he kissed her with pent-up feeling.

Annie, her pulse racing wildly now, felt his lips against her mouth and reeled with love for him. When he pulled away, she gazed up with raised eyebrows. Hadn't he heard what she'd admitted? "Jacob—"

"Ike can't—and never will—love you as much as I do."

Annie's heart beat with joy. "And that's why you kissed me?" she asked.

"You truly love me?" he said at the same time, apparently just realizing what she'd said.

Jacob gazed at the woman before him and longed to take her into his arms and prove to her that he would be a better husband than Ike or anyone. Hadn't he loved her since he was twelve? He had fought his feelings, shoved them to the back of his mind after she'd become his older brother Jed's sweetheart. He had known for years that she'd loved Jedidiah with all the passion of a young girl's heart, even before Jed had taken notice of her. But now that she was a woman, and he no longer a boy but a man, they could make it work if they both wanted it.

She didn't say anything at first as she inspected the box, turning it over to read the silly inscription he'd scratched into the metal bottom with a forged nail.

"I don't think anyone has ever made anything more lovely for me," she murmured as she looked up and met his gaze. "And to think that I never knew how you felt."

There was nothing mocking or teasing him about the box, no hint of rejection in her pretty blue eyes. She extended the container toward him, and when he reached for it, Annie grabbed his hand and pulled him close. The keepsake fell to the ground as she cupped his face and pressed her lips against his mouth.

"Jacob Lapp, what am I going to do with you?" she whispered.

Jacob stared at her, swallowed. "Love me?" he suggested hoarsely.

"I do." Annie smiled, warmth radiating from her in thick waves. "Jacob, I can't marry Ike King, even if he asks."

"Why?"

"Because he isn't you." She reached for his hand, raised it to examine the burn. "I was sorry when you hurt yourself. I wanted badly to make it feel better, but there was only so much I could do."

Jacob gazed at her bright face, wondering if he'd heard right when she'd said that she loved him. Had he been dreaming?

"Annie—"

"I love you, Jacob," she said, "and I know now that you love me."

Jacob smiled. "Only as much as a man can love a woman and more." He saw her eyes fill with tears. He frowned. "Annie, what's wrong?"

"I didn't understand. You kissed me and then avoided me."

He nodded as he settled his hands on her shoulders, as his gaze roamed over her lovely face, enjoying every glorious inch of it. She was everything to him. "I was afraid to hope," he admitted. "I wanted more from you, but you seemed determined to stick to your plan."

He heard her sigh.

He lifted a hand from her shoulder to caress her cheek. "Annie Zook, I want to court you and marry you." He frowned. "You will marry me?" She nodded, and he continued, "I don't have much to offer you now. But I will. I'll find a job quickly. I don't want to be apart from you any longer than necessary."

"I'll wait for as long as you need," she promised. "At least now, we know how we feel about each other." She looked as if she had something to say, but then she bit her lip instead. "Jacob, I think we should get back, although I would like nothing more than to be alone with you." He released her and she stepped back.

"Your *dat*—"

"Guessed we love each other." Annie grinned, and Jacob felt the sunshine warmth of her smile.

Walking with her by his side as they approached the house, Jacob felt the true power of God's blessings.

Annie halted suddenly. "Ike," she said.

"Do you want me to talk with him?" he asked. The day had turned cloudy. It looked as if it would rain.

"*Nay*, I should be the one to talk with him," she replied, glancing toward the farmhouse.

Ike was on the front porch talking with Horseshoe Joe.

A drop of moisture fell from the sky, hitting Annie on the nose. Annie glanced toward the darkening clouds. "*Dat* was right. He said it would rain." Her smile for him held love. "The shop window," she said and frowned. "What if *Dat* left it open?"

He touched her arm. "I'll go check," he said. His gaze

fell on Ike. "I'll be right back. Wait for me before you go up the house?"

"Ja." She appeared uneasy, as if she dreaded her confrontation with Ike King.

She was still standing where he'd left her when he returned.

"Things will be fine, Annie."

She sighed. "We both know what it's like to be hurt by someone. Ike and I weren't courting, but…"

Jacob focused his gaze on Ike and what he saw made him smile. "Ike will be fine. Look. He seems to have found someone who appears to be fascinated by him." He gestured toward Ike and the woman, who were deep in conversation. Jacob beamed a smile at Annie. "Isn't that Martha Shrock?"

"Ja." Annie returned his grin. "So it is. And she is perfect for Ike."

"Let's go. I need to speak with your *vadder*." He captured her hand, gave it a gentle squeeze, before he released it.

"I had no idea that you loved me," she whispered as if she still couldn't believe her good fortune as they walked toward the house.

"I didn't realize how affected you were by my kiss," he echoed. He grinned teasingly.

Annie's smile was warm, loving and joyful. "It was a kiss, nothing more."

He accepted her challenge. "You'd better be prepared for more of my kisses—and to marry me."

Annie beamed at him. "I'll marry you and love you forever."

He felt shaky at her declaration of love. He'd never expected to be given such a gift from Annie. Joe Zook rolled down his wheelchair ramp and into the yard.

"There's your *dat*," he said. He grabbed Annie's hand, not caring if everyone saw or what they might think. He loved Annie, and that's all that mattered. "I need to talk with him."

"I think he has something he wants to tell you, too," Annie said. Then, laughing, she ran to keep up with him when he hurried to talk with her father, and the joy in Jacob's heart filled to overflowing.

A while later, Annie asked, "Did my *vadder* talk with you?" She offered a tentative smile.

He nodded. *"Ja."* His expression gave nothing away.

Annie felt a sniggle of concern. "And?"

Jacob grinned suddenly, grabbed her about the waist and spun her around, with his laughter bubbling up to the surface. "I'll be staying to work at the blacksmithy!"

Annie felt breathless as he set her down. "You don't mind?" She stepped back and straightened her prayer *kapp*.

"Nay! I love the work." He gazed lovingly into her blue eyes as he ran his finger over her cheek and chin. "I love you, Anna Marie Zook."

The warmth in his expression, his words, melted her heart. "I love you, Jacob Lapp." She hesitated. "I didn't know how you'd feel about *Dat's* offer of a job. 'Tis not that we must wed in a hurry."

He scowled at her. "Why not wed in a hurry?"

"I—" The teasing gleam in his golden eyes made her giggle.

"I want to marry you now," he said earnestly.

She raised her eyebrows. "Now?"

"As soon as can be arranged."

"Will you marry me this November? I know we haven't courted long."

"I have known you for most of my life. I've been ready to marry you, Jacob, since I first realized I loved you."

"We should tell our parents—"

"No need to tell yours," Jacob said. "I've asked and been given permission by your parents to court and marry their daughter."

He opened his arms and she slipped into the haven of his embrace. He hugged her close, and Annie knew that her prayers had been answered in the best way possible.

"Where will we live?" she asked.

Jacob smiled. "I have an idea, but I can't tell you yet."

"As long as we're together, I'll be happy," she said. "Will you?"

"*Ja*, Jacob Lapp. You make me very happy."

Epilogue

September, a year later

Annie watched as her husband chased the little girl around the yard until he caught her. Jacob lifted the toddler high, and she giggled. He set her down, and she stumbled away from him laughing. Annie chuckled as she watched Jacob give chase and capture her all over again, much to the child's delight.

"You're going to tire her out before lunch," Annie called out.

"You'll eat before you nap, won't ya, Rachel?" Jacob asked the little girl. He bent down as if to hear the child's whisper. "She said she'll eat and then sleep," he assured his wife.

"But Joan will be coming for her soon." Annie cradled her large belly as she rose from a wooden chair out on the lawn behind their new home. They had lived in the schoolhouse until their house was finished. "She'll expect our niece to have eaten." Her sister and her husband had moved back to Lancaster County, much to the family's delight.

Jacob pouted. Annie laughed as she waddled in his

direction. He stood still, his expression warming as he watched her approach. "You look more beautiful every day," he murmured.

Annie beamed at him. "I grow bigger every day."

"Ja," Jacob agreed, "but I couldn't be happier." He placed a hand on her belly. "He moved!" he exclaimed with delight.

She chuckled. "Thank the Lord," she said.

"You've made me happy, Annie, happier than I could have ever imagined." He frowned suddenly as he looked for his niece. When he found her, he grinned and pointed. "I think Rachel decided to take her nap *before* lunch."

Following his direction, Annie saw her little niece curled up on the grass with her eyes closed. "So she did." She smiled affectionately at Jacob. "Do you want to carry her inside or should I?"

He raised his eyebrows. "Not in your condition."

Amused, she watched him tenderly pick up their niece. Jacob had confided that he wanted as many children as she. This wasn't the time, she decided, to remind him that there would be occasions when she'd be large with child, with a little one on her hip. *Jacob, my wonderful husband, will be a* gut vadder. He had made her world complete.

Inside the house, he placed the little girl on their bed. He rose and then met her gaze. "Annie?"

"I love you, Jacob. I'll love you forever."

His golden eyes glowed as he slipped his arms around her. "I love you, Annie, and I will love you beyond my last breath."

* * * * *

Dear Reader,

I'm happy that you've decided to visit Happiness in Lancaster County, Pennsylvania, home to several Amish families who are characters in my Lancaster County Weddings series.

Hurt by love in the past, Annie Zook has decided to avoid the risk of heartbreak by marrying an older man in her church community, someone who will appreciate her and offer her a safe kind of love. Jacob liked Annie when he was a young boy, but Annie preferred his older brother Jedidiah. Despite her and Jed's breakup, Annie clearly still has feelings for Jed. Jacob gave up on his feelings for Annie long ago. But after Horseshoe Joe, Annie's father, suffers an accident, circumstances throw Annie and Jacob into each other's company and a friendship develops between them. As their feelings toward each other grow, Annie and Jacob stay determined to protect their hearts and keep their feelings for each other hidden.

Annie and Jacob will learn that love isn't something that can be planned or controlled. Love is a gift. Love is God, and by loving another, one knows God.

I hope you enjoy Annie and Jacob's story and that you will return to my little Happiness Amish community another time to learn how Jacob's siblings discover love.

Blessings and light,
Rebecca Kertz

REQUEST YOUR FREE BOOKS!

2 FREE INSPIRATIONAL NOVELS
PLUS 2
FREE
MYSTERY GIFTS

Love Inspired

YES! Please send me 2 FREE Love Inspired® novels and my 2 FREE mystery gifts (gifts are worth about $10). After receiving them, if I don't wish to receive any more books, I can return the shipping statement marked "cancel." If I don't cancel, I will receive 6 brand-new novels every month and be billed just $4.74 per book in the U.S. or $5.24 per book in Canada. That's a saving of at least 21% off the cover price. It's quite a bargain! Shipping and handling is just 50¢ per book in the U.S. and 75¢ per book in Canada.* I understand that accepting the 2 free books and gifts places me under no obligation to buy anything. I can always return a shipment and cancel at any time. Even if I never buy another book, the two free books and gifts are mine to keep forever.

105/305 IDN F47Y

Name   (PLEASE PRINT)

Address   Apt. #

City   State/Prov.   Zip/Postal Code

Signature (if under 18, a parent or guardian must sign)

Mail to the **Harlequin® Reader Service:**
IN U.S.A.: P.O. Box 1867, Buffalo, NY 14240-1867
IN CANADA: P.O. Box 609, Fort Erie, Ontario L2A 5X3

**Are you a subscriber to Love Inspired books
and want to receive the larger-print edition?
Call 1-800-873-8635 or visit www.ReaderService.com.**

* Terms and prices subject to change without notice. Prices do not include applicable taxes. Sales tax applicable in N.Y. Canadian residents will be charged applicable taxes. Offer not valid in Quebec. This offer is limited to one order per household. Not valid for current subscribers to Love Inspired books. All orders subject to credit approval. Credit or debit balances in a customer's account(s) may be offset by any other outstanding balance owed by or to the customer. Please allow 4 to 6 weeks for delivery. Offer available while quantities last.

Your Privacy—The Harlequin® Reader Service is committed to protecting your privacy. Our Privacy Policy is available online at www.ReaderService.com or upon request from the Harlequin Reader Service.

We make a portion of our mailing list available to reputable third parties that offer products we believe may interest you. If you prefer that we not exchange your name with third parties, or if you wish to clarify or modify your communication preferences, please visit us at www.ReaderService.com/consumerchoice or write to us at Harlequin Reader Service Preference Service, P.O. Box 9062, Buffalo, NY 14269. Include your complete name and address.

LI13R

SPECIAL EXCERPT FROM

Love Inspired

Can Mary find happiness with a secretive stranger who saves her life?

Read on for a sneak preview of the final book in Patricia Davids's **BRIDES OF AMISH COUNTRY** *series,* **AMISH REDEMPTION**.

Hannah edged closer to her. "I don't like storms."

Mary slipped an arm around her daughter. "Don't worry. We'll be at Katie's house before the rain catches us."

It turned out she was wrong. Big raindrops began hitting her windshield. A strong gust of wind shook the buggy and blew dust across the road. The sky grew darker by the minute. She urged Tilly to a faster pace. She should have stayed home.

A red car flew past her with the driver laying on the horn. Tilly shied and nearly dragged the buggy into the fence along the side of the road. Mary managed to right her. "Foolish *Englischers*. We are over as far as we can get."

The rumble of thunder became a steady roar behind them. Tilly broke into a run. Hannah began screaming. Mary glanced back and her heart stopped. A tornado had dropped from the clouds and was bearing down on them. Dust and debris flew out from the wide base.

Dear God, help me save my baby. What do I do?

She saw an intersection up ahead.

Bracing her legs against the dash, she pulled back on the lines, trying to slow Tilly enough to make the corner without overturning. The mare seemed to sense the plan. She slowed and made the turn with the buggy tilting on two wheels. Mary grabbed Hannah and held on to her. Swerving wildly behind the horse, the buggy finally came back onto all four wheels. Before the mare could gather speed again, a man jumped into the road waving his arms. He grabbed Tilly's bridle and pulled her to a stop.

Shouting, he pointed toward an abandoned farmhouse. "There's a cellar on the south side."

Mary jumped out of the buggy and pulled Hannah into her arms. The man was already unhitching Tilly, so Mary ran toward the ramshackle structure. The wind threatened to pull her off her feet. The trees and even the grass were straining toward the approaching tornado. She reached the old cellar door, but couldn't lift it against the force of the wind. She was about to lie on the ground on top of Hannah when the man appeared at her side. Together, they were able to lift the door.

A second later, she was pushed down the steps into darkness.

Don't miss
AMISH REDEMPTION by Patricia Davids,
available April 2015 wherever
Love Inspired® books and ebooks are sold.

www.Harlequin.com